A Testimony of Lions

By
Robert M. Otis

ISBN 0-7414-3803-8

COVER DESIGN: Robert Otis and Lynda Wise

PHOTO CREDIT: The photograph on the cover of the Lion's Gate was used by permission of Holy Land Photos.

Published by:

INFI∞ITY
PUBLISHING.COM

1094 New DeHaven Street, Suite 100
West Conshohocken, PA 19428-2713
Info@buybooksontheweb.com
www.buybooksontheweb.com
Toll-free (877) BUY BOOK
Local Phone (610) 941-9999
Fax (610) 941-9959

Printed in the United States of America

Printed on Recycled Paper

Published October 2007

TO LYNDA

FOREWORD

I read very few fiction books, so when my friend, Bob Otis, asked me to edit and read his book, *A Testimony of Lions*, I was a bit apprehensive. As I was reading the book for the first time, concentrating on the editing work, I was constantly drawn, time and place, into the intriguing plot. After finishing the editing, I couldn't help but read the book again. At every twist and turn of each historical and archaeological fact, (is this really fiction?), I found myself wanting to know more; desiring the truth for a decision that would ultimately have to be made. The Testimony of Lions demands it and you cannot help yourself from making it...a decision that may change your life for eternity.

A Testimony of Lions is a book you will not be able to put down, nor will you want to. It will touch every part of you; physically, emotionally and spiritually. You will enjoy the intense impact.

I can hardly wait to feel and read this wonderful book a third time!

In His service;
Jim Wise
Entrepreneur
Greedy for God

The story in this book has no more to do with living lions than "A FISH CALLED WANDA" had to do with the study of marine life. You will, however, find the title very significant as it relates to the story.

THE YEAR IS 1984.

CHAPTER I

Felix Renthroe sat tapping his fingers to an uneven cadence on the briefcase still chained to his wrist. He was making a conscious effort not to fidget in his chair. He could feel the dampness beginning to form under his arms, soaking his shirt. He didn't mind that as much as he did the way it stained his shoulder holster.

Felix was rather nondescript in appearance, which was an asset in his line of work. Average height, average weight, thinning brown hair, with a face that could easily get lost in a crowd. Right now he looked a little older than his forty-three years, suffering from fatigue, confusion, jet lag, indigestion and anxiety. Three of the five were occupational hazards, but confusion was a twist that didn't usually enter into his assignments. Normally, anxiety wasn't a factor either because his boss usually handled these briefings. However, Stan was in El Salvador and even though Felix had been at a private conference before, he still felt a little ill at ease when briefing the President of the United States.

He was not intimidated or even awed by the office. Encounters with world leaders had become commonplace to him, and in their last meeting the President had quickly put him at ease. So why all the anxiety? It was the confusion, he was sure. Here he was, about to brief the President on a matter of national security, and he wasn't at all sure he knew what the hell he was talking about.

He had helped edit almost every briefing paper his boss, Stan Wyman, Director of the C.I.A. had ever presented to the President in their regularly scheduled meetings. Felix's job was to cut through the crap, give the verifiable facts, analyze the credible speculation, outline the ramifications, probabilities and possibilities and then suggest a course of action including alternatives and possible repercussions.

How he wished Stan were here. This was unlike anything he had ever dealt with before. This one actually scared him. How could it have happened? How did it get by everybody? And without even trying.

Two days ago he had received a call from Chris Cagney, Director of Operations with N.A.S.A. in Houston. He suggested they meet as soon as possible with a Dr. Wendell Perry, at Cal Tech in Pasadena. Chris was hesitant to fill him in on anything, not even trusting the phone scrambler. Felix knew that Chris was not an alarmist, so when he said "as soon as possible," Felix found himself strapping on a seat belt for a landing at L.A.X. six hours later.

Chris was waiting for him at a back booth of a Denny's on Sepulveda Boulevard. His close cropped, prematurely gray hair made his well tanned face look even darker. Felix thought he looked several years older than he did ten months ago when they had dinner together in Washington. Maybe he'd been working too hard.

Chris butted his cigarette out when he saw Felix approach. Forcing a smile, he rose halfway out of his seat and extended his hand.

"Howdy, G-Man."

"Hi ya, Flash. How are things on Mongo?"

"Thanks for coming."

"The tone in your voice told me I didn't have much choice."

"Did I sound that bad?"

"Well, let me put it this way: I'm half afraid to ask you what this is all about."

"You and I are going to find out together from Dr. Perry. I'll tell you all I know so far, but it appears that we'll be dealing with a bunch of unknowns, which is more down your alley than mine. Anyway, that's why I wanted you in on this from the beginning."

"So, it's the beginning. What's going on? Are we on a collision course with another planet?"

"You've been watching too many old movies. Truth of the matter is, we've got a man and a piece of equipment missing," he paused a second and drew a deep breath, "and the way it looks right now, he's been able to put himself into a different place in time."

Felix only stared at him while he let the statement sink in.

"And you think I've been watching too many old movies?"

Cagney's face was devoid of any humor as he spoke. "I've known Wendell Perry for years and he's not a man to be taken lightly, nor is he the type to be involved in, or easily fooled by, some hoax."

"My God, Chris, I knew you guys were messing with some pretty far out projects, but I really thought that sort of stuff could only be accomplished at Universal Studios."

"Apparently, so did a lot of us."

"What do you mean?"

"I mean we're talking about a project that has been funded for nearly seventeen years, right under our noses. It was a subject we couldn't completely ignore, mainly because the Russians have a similar project in Budapest. It was basically a one-man show, with a budget so small it wasn't worth cutting even when Congress was breathing hard for us to sharpen our scissors. But nobody, damn it all," he paused, shaking his head and staring straight ahead, "nobody really took it seriously."

A waitress came up, apologizing for not having seen him come in, and handed him a menu.

"Just coffee." This time it was Felix who forced the smile.

She turned a cup over and poured from the pot she carried with her. She refilled Chris' cup, laid down a separate check, and left.

3

"O.K.", Felix began, interrupting himself with a sip of coffee. "First things first: Who is this guy and what do we have on him?"

"I pulled the file on him before I left Houston and from all indications he seems to be one of your more normal geniuses. His name is Eric Corbett. He's a healthy, good looking guy, forty-seven years old, a practicing heterosexual with no known peculiar tastes or habits. He's never been married. Lives modestly and has never displayed an appetite for expensive material things. He'd like to see a lot of things done differently by our government, but doesn't believe that the country should be scrapped and started over again from scratch. Almost no family except for a sister in Portland. Well liked, but no really close friends unless you'd count Wendell Perry, and that's about it. Oh yes, on his last psychological profile interview, submitted three months ago, it was noted that the only recognizable change from prior interviews was a detectable increase of interest on the subject of religion."

Chris stopped and blew on the coffee the waitress had just poured. "You're welcome to the file if you think his place of birth, parents' background, schooling, service record and all that other good stuff will help you before talking to Perry."

"No." Felix said, "There will be plenty of time for that later. What about this piece of equipment that's missing with him?"

"Well," Chris lit another cigarette, "for want of a better description, I guess you might call it a Time Machine."

"Damn it all, Chris," Felix raised his voice then brought it back down to a whisper, remembering where he was, "how in the hell is this even possible? I mean, here's a guy working all alone on a budget that wouldn't keep most of your departments in paper clips, and he comes up with a machine that, as far as I'm concerned, is even more mind boggling than all that trillion dollar's worth of hardware we've got cluttering up the moon."

4

"I know, I know." Chris began to get irritated. "Let's wait until we have a few more facts before we start concerning ourselves with the 'where did we go wrong' questions."

"Sorry, Chris. I know you haven't had time to check this thing out yet."

"Now that this has come up," Chris said, cupping his chin, "I do recall a rather large hardware item that I approved on a requisition for Wendell a couple of months ago. It was $115,000 for a vacuum tube and an electronic gyroscope. That's pocket change for what normally runs across my desk, but it was a very large expenditure for them. In fact, I meant to call him about it, but it happened on one of those days with only twenty-four hours in it." "Yeah, I know, I hate that kind, too. There's never enough time to get anything done."

This time they both managed a weak smile because they could relate to each other's schedules.

"What in hell is an electronic gyroscope?" Felix asked.

"The truth is, that's the reason I was going to call, because I don't know either. I mean, gyros are the heart of all of our guidance systems, but they're all mechanical. I thought maybe it was just a typographical error, especially since it was just a general heading that listed a bunch of components... I'm sure that whatever it was, Corbett planned on building it himself."

"What did this thing look like, Chris?"

"According to Perry, it resembled the cockpit of a miniature helicopter."

"And you're sure there's no way this guy, or somebody else, for that matter, could have gotten that thing out of there, either assembled or broken down?"

"The security in that place would have put Los Alamos to shame. They're right down to the voice prints and the body temperature. You couldn't get a pencil sharpener out of there without a Presidential order."

"There's a guy I know in Warsaw who could steal your contact lenses while he's talking to you and you'd never know they're gone." Felix wished he had left that unsaid.

"O.K., G-Man, that's why you're here," Chris said. "You figure out the answers. After all, what do I know except how to fly a rocket?"

"Ya know, Chris, we gotta have lunch one of these days so you can teach me how to do that."

"I'll be happy to, but only if you promise to teach me everything you know about national security the next time we go to the head."

"Touché"

"My God," Chris said, "the most significant scientific development since the atomic bomb is missing and we're sitting here doing Rowan and Martin."

"My daddy once told me that the only deterrent to insanity was a little nonsense," Felix quipped.

Chris rolled his eyes at the corny philosophy.

"O.K., just two more questions before we go see Perry."

"Shoot."

"If he did it, how in the hell did he do it?"

"I knew you were going to get around to that, but we're going to have to save that for Perry. Hell, Felix, as far as I know this guy has rewritten every law of physics we've ever known. He left his files there, but Perry believes we're missing the last page of some important equations."

"How important?"

"The kind that could take years. But it's too soon to tell."

"Last question. Who all knows about this?"

"As far as I know, just Perry and a paleontologist named Dorene Schueler who was the one who reported to Perry that Corbett's machine was missing. Possibly a maintenance man named Sanchez, but all of them have Top Secret clearance."

"We'll order an immediate surveillance on them."

"What in hell for? They've been told to say nothing. I mean, why bother to clear them if you can't trust them?"

"That's the most important thing you'll ever learn about national security, Chris. Trust no one. As soon as you've

6

assured me that this thing doesn't represent a threat to our security, then I'll treat it as such, but for now what we have is so unbelievable that I can't even think of the right questions... even if you had the answers."

The moment got very serious as both men stared across the table at each other.

Felix lightened things by saying, "O.K., let's go see Perry. But first, one more question."

"I thought you said two questions ago, only two more?"

"I lied."

"O.K., what's the question?"

"Are you buying the coffee?"

"No."

"This generosity from a man with a billion dollar budget?"

"My daddy always said, 'Waste not, want not.'"

"No more daddy jokes. Let's go to Pasadena."

The gray unmarked car turned onto the Cal Tech campus. It pulled into the parking lot of a small building identified only by a small sign that read, "N.A.S.A. Rand Corporation Affiliate." Stopping in a visitor's parking area, Felix and Chris got out and noticed a security guard sitting in a car next to another one that had been cordoned off with yellow POLICE ONLY tape. They walked over and identified themselves. The guard could only tell them that the car was unlocked and the keys still in the ignition. His only instructions were to guard the car. The name on the assigned space read CORBETT.

They walked around to the main entrance and entered the building. The lobby was large and immaculately clean, but it lacked any warmth. There were no pictures or plaques or even trade magazines to give a visitor any clue as to what went on there. The furnishings in the room were obviously not designed for high traffic, yet there were three security guards behind a counter that contained panels of T.V.

monitors. These weren't your garden variety guards like the one in the parking lot. They were young, fit, and appeared to be highly trained.

One of the guards greeted them with military politeness and got on the intercom. In a few seconds another guard appeared from behind the only other door to the lobby and greeted them with equal courtesy, asking for identification. They walked to the security door where Chris put his card into a slot and placed his hand on a print scanner. The guard entered his card into the slot above. The door opened and the three men entered the hallway on the other side. The guard stopped and knocked on the second door on the left. A voice could be heard from the other side: "Come in."

The guard opened the door and allowed the two men to enter. Then with a polite smile he left, closing the door behind him.

Chris and Felix stood silently watching the small man in a white lab coat with his back to them scribble equations on a chalkboard. He would write a while and then suddenly pause, then just as suddenly start writing feverishly again, scribbling symbols that meant nothing to either of the intruders, in spite of the gravity of the situation, for the few seconds they stood there watching, the whole scene seemed to Felix to take on a cartoon effect.

Seconds later the writer slammed down his chalk in disgust, sighed and turned to his visitors. As he came across the room, extending his hand to Chris, a broad smile softened his face, making him look like an aging pixie.

"Hello, Chris. I've been expecting you."

"How are you, Wendell? Anything wrong?" Chris nodded toward the chalkboard.

"No, no; just another damn dead end."

"Dr. Wendell Perry, I'd like you to meet Felix Renthroe, Assistant Director of the C.I. A."

Shaking Felix's hand and making a gesture of playful guilt Wendell said, "We must be in bigger trouble than I thought to rate such high level investigation."

"That's what we're hoping you can tell us, Doctor," Felix replied.

His cherubic features were as quick to frown as they were to smile when his mood shifted with sudden concern, transforming him back into an old man. "I don't know how he did it," he said softly, with a pained expression. "I know where he made the turn, but to follow the equation out...I mean, everyone in his field had their hopes pinned on the cyclotron."

"The what?" Felix asked.

"A cyclotron! A process where an atomic accelerator shoots particles with velocities of millions of electron volts into a powerful magnetic field between two electrodes, moving them with increasing speed in a spiral path...you see, Einstein held that matter could not obtain the speed of light without reaching the ultimate mass...stopping even time...but Eric has unlocked it through a different equation without the use of massive hardware. Somehow he has doubled the speed of light and concentrated the energy onto a directable path."

"I'm afraid I don't understand, Doctor."

"Don't you see? Time and space are simply measurements of each other. We know that light itself is matter because its course is altered when it passes a gravitational field. There is speculation about objects at the outer most regions of the universe nearing light speed, but the unified field has yet to be established, so with what is presently at our disposal, if an object could travel even one mile per hour faster than the speed of light...would not time, as we know it, begin to reverse itself?"

Felix gave a bewildered glance to Chris. "Dr. Perry, you're talking to a guy who got a C-minus in algebra. My primary concern at the moment is about this man Corbett and how what he alone knows may affect our national security."

"What do you want to know about him?" Perry asked.

"Anything you can tell me. Chris said something about a note he left you."

Dr. Perry walked over to his desk, took an envelope out of the top drawer and handed it to Felix. It was a single page, hand written note, which Felix read quickly.

"Well, Dr. Perry, this completely exonerates you from having any knowledge of what he was about to do, but here's the part that interests me:" Felix read from the note, " 'Remember the night of the great Perry/Corbett debate? The one point we agreed upon was that science would come to an end when there were no longer any questions left to answer. Well, I think I've heard most of it from this end now, but there is another point of view I'd still like to hear. The odds aren't that great on getting an appointment - but I've got to try.' What did he mean by that?"

"I'm afraid, Mr. Renthroe, that your guess is as good as mine."

"What was the great debate he mentioned?"

"It was nothing, really; just another of those long, 'go no where' conversations about a subject matter to which there is no solution or resolution."

"It seemed important enough for him to mention. It could mean something. Mind telling me about it?"

Dr. Perry walked over to a filing cabinet and took down a tall glass candy jar filled with long twisted licorice sticks. He pulled out a piece and offered the jar to his guests who both refused. He rolled his eyes but offered no excuse for his childhood passion. He then settled into the chair behind his desk and appeared to go deep into thought as he prepared to take the two men on a verbal journey.

"The party was at Susan Garret's apartment. She's a darling little Ph.D. in Microbiology. You know, gentlemen, once in a while even we like to stop dreaming up insane methods of destroying, or keeping ourselves from destroying, this planet and just get drunk like other irrational people."

With that his face softened. He snapped off a piece of licorice and began giving them a running account of his discussion with Eric Corbett.

"Well now, first of all, gentlemen, you've got to under-stand that I believe Eric to have one of the finest minds in the scientific world. It's only been in the last few months that he's been acting a little strange."

"Could you explain that, Doctor?" Felix asked.

"Well, maybe strange isn't the word; perhaps illogical would be more accurate. It's like he expected his world of science to answer the questions that were really only ever meant for the philosophers of this world. We had sort of drifted away from the party out onto Susan's little upstairs sundeck. Now, I'll admit that the wine was flowing pretty good that night. In fact, Eric nearly spilled his when I slapped the railing we were leaning on and shouted, 'Poof!'"

"'Poof!,' Dr. Perry?" Felix asked.

"You've got to be kidding. Poof! Just like that...Hey guys, look, I've made man."

"Ya know, Wendell," Eric said, "it seems like ever since old Darwin wrote down some of his highly speculative and ever changing theories on how we got here, scientists and educators have been doing their best to make any other alternative seem as unsophisticated as you just tried to dramatize."

"Well, isn't that what the book said? He took some dirt and made a man."

"Not exactly. First there had to be dirt."

"Ah, come on, Eric."

"Hey, all I'm saying is that the first words in that book are: 'In the beginning God created the heavens and earth,' period. It didn't say how long ago, or what the procedure was; it just made that simple statement."

"Sounds like a cop out. Why couldn't he have told us a little bit about how he did it?"

"Oh sure, Wendell, this book tries to communicate some history and lessons about right and wrong to a bunch of people who are still in awe of the wheel and you want it to tell them about atoms and molecules."

"I take it, then, that you don't agree with the Lemaitres theory?"

"I'm not sure they conflict. Of course, the universe is expanding and quite possibly at one time all matter in the universe was confined in one primeval mass before the explosion that scattered it. But what we don't know is how the matter and the energy got there, and why."

"Oh, Eric, for God's sake, let's get another drink."

"Now wait a minute, Wendell, damn it all, neither an atom nor the universe is chaotic in nature. They are both orderly and function by laws that govern their behavior. Things that we keep learning in science about nature continue to amaze us and yet we are only learning about them, we didn't cause them to be. We just marvel at our own intelligence for having unlocked one of the mysteries that someone or something has put into effect to make things the way they are."

"Eric, where are you going with all of this?"

"Right down a dead end road, because nobody can hand anybody else the answer. I was only trying to get you to leave some doors open."

"I'm not a hard head, it's just that magic wands are not what I look to for answers."

"Have it your way, magic wands or guiding force, but then just tell me, with all of this matter and energy speeding outward, who came up with the plan of a thing called gravity that would pull all of these particles together and form stars in galaxies that would form solar systems that would one day cool down and produce the conditions for a single cell to develop and give life to itself and multiply and ooze out of the mud so you and I could make our way to this porch and get drunk."

"No one ever said that we had all the answers. But we have progressed somewhat since the invention of the wheel and now it's simply that knowledge and logic have replaced superstition."

"O.K., let's talk logic. To say that the cell designed itself would be like saying that New York was built without architects, even if you had all of the materials and laborers. Is that logical?"

"Your hypothesis is growing absurd."

"It does seem absurd that man's technology can put a man on the moon but we can't make a blade of grass or a trilobite."

"What are you after here, the origin of living matter? No one will ever pinpoint that phenomenon for you."

"All right, then, let's set that little mystery on a back burner and say that it 'just happened.' But let's take that miraculous lonely little cell and see what it had to accomplish by trial and error 'natural selection,' if you will."

"Well, since it seems to be soap box time, why don't you go ahead and give me your theory or its underpinnings."

"Since a theory is an opinion not yet verified by documentable fact, I can only give you a speculative assumption that somewhere along the line, without reason or guidance, this little darling divided itself and began to multiply. Now, according to some of our N.A.S.A. sponsored brothers at Ames Research, in Mountain View, they just discovered last year that life began in clay and not in the sea. They said clay contains the two basic properties essential to life: to store and transfer energy coming from radioactive decay. This formed 'chemical factories' which processed inorganic raw materials into the more complex molecules from which the first life arose."

"So, what's your point?"

"No real point here except maybe your crack about 'hey guys, look what I just made out of dirt.'"

"Oh come now, that wasn't what I meant."

"I know, I know. I'm only trying to point out that the laws of 'nature,' if you will, are constant and unchanging, but man keeps making new discoveries about them, then announcing to the world, 'Now this is how it really happened.'"

"What would you have us do; not think? Not question?"

"Of course not, but why is science so determined to establish a conflict with creationists. Two years ago you would have maintained that ole Moses should have written in Genesis that God took some sea water and made a man; but now it seems that maybe it was O.K. for him to have used dirt."

"Dirt, water, or soy beans, what's the difference? Is this your idea of convincing logic?"

"Actually, it has nothing to do with it. But, if you will concede to me that the existence of the light bulb would be highly improbable without the efforts of Thomas Edison, I'll try to make my point."

"Come on, Eric, that's one of those silly little trick questions. If Edison hadn't come up with it somebody else would have later on."

"My point isn't who. My point is that it didn't just happen. Somebody had to plan it, design it, make it work."

"I don't consider that observation to be overwhelming."

"You don't find it overwhelming to believe that thought had to go into the running of current through wires inside a vacuum of glass to create light, but yet you find it believable that a live cell could create itself and determine that it should become a molecule and that this molecule would develop a D.N.A. process that would determine what form it should take. Did it decide what organs it should have: heart, lungs, gills, bones? Or what senses: sight, smell, hearing? How does a creature simple develop an eye if it doesn't even know what vision is? And all of these things that had to have taken place for man to evolve just happened without some kind of Thomas Edison behind it."

"Well, nobody said it happened in seven days. It took billions of years."

"You're asking me to believe that if you shook up all of the compound nuts and bolts of an automobile for a billion years that someday they'd all fall into place and make a Chevrolet?"

"Is this going to become a comedy take off of an intellectual discussion?"

"I'm only trying to point out that a hell of a lot of accidental things had to have taken place for atoms to have pulled together to form ninety two elements that could combine into compounds and form cells and molecules that would engineer itself into the complexity of the human brain."

"Eric, do you really expect Science to have answers to all the questions that exist in the universe?"

"No, but until it does I'd like to see Science ease off of this pompous rigidity that implies that someday we'll have the answers to evolution, because the idea of creation, or at least a causing force, is only to be believed by old ladies and unenlightened people still clinging to a belief in something they call a creator."

"There are no answers to the questions you ask, anymore than there are to the old time-honored question of 'where did God come from?' The answer you always get is that God simply 'always was.' Well, I say to you that matter and energy simply 'always were.'"

"Sold. Except you left out two important factors: They both have orderly behavior that combined to somehow transcend from inorganic to organic."

"Eric, could you accept an Agnostic's confession that I am not a hard core atheist, but what are you trying to get me to say, that God provided the orderly behavior and the transition from dead to living matter?"

"That wouldn't serve any purpose to either of us, Wendell. This isn't a win/lose subject. But if we've boiled it down to matter and energy having always existed, or matter and energy with a directing force of orderly behavior, then I'm going to have to go with the latter...and wonder who, or what, provided it."

"O.K., O.K. I've had a little too much wine to tell if you've done it with fancy words or with logic, but for the sake of a merciful conclusion, let's say I buy your final point...where does that leave it?"

"With the biggest question of all," Eric sighed.

"Which is?"

"Why?"

"Oh for God's sake, Eric, give me a break! Let's get another drink." Dr. Perry started to get up.

"What's so illogical about that?"

"You give me half an hour of rhetoric with just enough sense to it that I'm ready to admit that just maybe there is some sort of 'Master Engineer' behind the whole scheme of things, but then you want to ask some stupid question like why."

"But don't you see, Wendell, that if there is order, and this third little planet out from the Sun did bloom with life, there must be a purpose, a reason, a plan."

Still standing, Dr. Perry raised his nearly empty glass in a toast, "Well, my friend, if you ever come up with that answer I'd like very much to resume this conversation."

There was just a shadow of a strange look on Corbett's face when he said, "Maybe we'll just do that."

Several seconds went by before Felix spoke. "Tell me, Doctor, do you see any connection between that conversation and Corbett's disappearance?"

"I have no idea. As you can see, it was just another of those 'never to be resolved' conversations. Religion and politics; the two subjects everyone always claims they never discuss but, somehow, never seem to avoid."

CHAPTER II

After sixteen hours in Pasadena, including six with Dr. Perry, and three hours of fitful sleep on a bumpy flight from Los Angeles, Felix found himself fidgeting in a high back chair in Washington, at 10:00 at night, all alone outside the President's office. He was still uncomfortable because of all the unknowns that were dangling, especially in the area of the ability to alter events which have already happened. It didn't seem possible, for the simple reason that they had already happened. And yet, what would have been the course of world events if Bonaparte's mother had died prior to giving him birth? In the past several hours Felix had wrestled with hundreds of hypothetical situations which had left him exhausted because there were no answers. This whole thing was so bizarre he still couldn't believe it was happening. To top it all off, he had absolutely no input pertaining to Soviet intelligence, position, action, or reaction.

Relax, he told himself. After all, you didn't invent this situation, you're only reporting it.

At ten o'clock exactly, Ruth Evans, the President's secretary, opened the door. She greeted Felix with a warm, but tired smile as she showed him into the Oval Office. He instantly recognized Doug Wakefield, the Secretary of State, and Max Greer, the Secretary of Defense. As Felix approached the large desk the President stood up, extended his hand, and flashed a warm, familiar smile that probably had a great deal to do with his being elected. He was a tall, handsome man that looked much younger than his years. Even so, Felix could see in his face the toll that the pressures of the office had taken in the three years since he had coordinated security with the Secret Service during the last election campaign.

"Good to see you again, Felix," the President said. "You know Max Greer, a retired General, was a former member of the Joint Chiefs of Staff. A barrel-chested man with hawk-like features, he looked strangely out of place in civilian clothes.

Doug Wakefield was almost the total opposite of Greer. A soft, kind face mounted on top of an obviously out of shape body. He used his power in a gentle way without beating you over the head with it. Not only was this his manner, but it was a luxury he could well afford since he was unquestionably the President's right hand man and everybody in Washington, right down to the Pages, knew it.

"Can I offer you something, Felix?" the President asked.

"No, thank you, sir."

Another pleasant smile and a nod from the President dismissed Ruth and she closed the door behind her.

"I've got to tell you something, Felix," the President began. "You're the only person requesting a priority appointment who actually scares me. You know I see Stan Wyman at least once a week on routine briefings, so when you've got something that won't keep until Stan gets back I figure we've really got a problem. I seem to recall," he continued, almost as if he were trying to postpone hearing whatever it was Felix might have to say, "that the last time you were here it was to tell me about a Russian satellite loaded with radioactive material that was plummeting out of control and falling to earth. You're not going to lay something like that on me again, are you?"

"No, Mr. President, nothing like that. What we have now is far more difficult to analyze, but may or may not offer any threat to national security."

"What's going on, Felix?"

"Well, sir, it appears that one of our N.A.S.A. R and D Labs has developed a piece of equipment that can place material objects into a different time, a time other than the one we're in right now."

There was a long period of silence while the three men looked at each other as if to confirm that they had all heard the same thing.

"You mean, like a time machine?" Doug Wakefield asked.

"Yes, sir."

Again silence.

"Son of a bitch."

Felix had never heard the President use profanity before and it caught him off guard.

The President clapped his hands together and was smiling from ear to ear. His tired face took on a youthful appearance.

"That's been a fantasy of mine since I was a little kid," he said, getting up and walking around his desk. "How does it work?"

"Well, sir, that's part of the problem. We're not really sure."

"What's that supposed to mean, Felix? Did we build the damn thing or not?"

"Well, yes sir." Felix began to squirm a little. "But it seems that it was basically a one-man project, and now the man and the equipment are missing."

"Missing?" The President asked, his moment of joy fading rapidly.

"Yes, sir. From everything we've been able to compile so far, it appears that this man decided to use himself as the guinea pig on an unauthorized maiden experiment. We have reason to believe that he has gone backward into time, possibly in an attempt to witness some religious event. We have no idea what success he had. But the point is, we are 99% convinced that he was able to move himself and the capsule into a different dimension or time frame."

"And the other 1%?" the President asked.

"A hoax, sir. But my feelings don't even really give it a 1%. We are, of course, checking it out."

"Damn it all, Felix," Max Greer bellowed, "how is that possible? This isn't some James Bond movie where one man steals a rocket ship. It takes hundreds of people to coordinate those things. Are you telling us that this guy just walks into his lab one night and decides to take a little ride?"

19

"Impossible as it sounds, Mr. Secretary, your analogy is probably pretty close to exactly what happened."

"Felix, you said you weren't sure whether or not this incident could affect our national security. Please explain," Doug Wakefield asked.

"Well, sir, we all know that the actions we take today are what shape the events of tomorrow. But what we don't know is whether an event that has already happened can be changed to occur in a different way or even not occur at all. For example, let me select a subject that may be a little dramatic, so much so that it's probably been the subject matter of a dozen or more old sci-fi movies or T.V. plots, but I'm sure you'll see my point.

"Because the end results would justify the means," Felix knew he had chosen a subject that was never discussed in open meetings, even as intimate as the one they were in, "if the decision were made to temporarily alter our national policy on assassination, suppose we were to use a machine like this to transport an assassination squad back into the year 1930. The death of some loud-mouthed paperhanger with political ambitions would probably only make the back page of the local Berlin newspaper. But without Adolf Hitler, would there have been a World War II? For additional insurance, we mark Goebbels, Goering, Himmler or anyone else who had the potential to carry off what Hitler did."

"My God, is that possible, Felix?" the President asked.

"We don't know, sir, but we have to consider it a possibility."

"Can you imagine the Russians' reactions if they thought we had advanced information on grain harvests, oil field locations, missile sites and capabilities, world currency and gold fixes. This whole thing is just too unbelievable." Doug Wakefield was shaking his head as some of the ramifications began to be clear to him.

"How many people know about this, Felix?" the President asked.

"Except for the people in this room, we believe only four other people and, of course, Corbett."

"Who?"

"Oh, I'm sorry, sir. Eric Corbett. He's the missing physicist who's handed us this hot potato."

"What does his psychological profile look like?" Greer asked.

"Well, Mr. Secretary, that's the one bright spot in the picture. Corbett is so well adjusted it's almost boring. There wasn't a kinky, wild-eyed incident to be found anywhere."

"O.K. now, Felix," The President began," I'm going to ask the near impossible of you. But then, I'm sure you didn't expect anything less."

Felix managed another one of his forced smiles.

"First of all, I want you to slam a lid on this like you've never slammed before. At the same time, I want you to find out if the K.G.B. even has a smell of anything. Optimum discretion is the key here. I want you to take personal charge of the operation until we find out what we're dealing with. I also want you to use every means possible, no holds barred, to locate or verify the whereabouts of this man Corbett. You'll report directly to me on any new developments. I'll clear it with Stan."

"Is there any way we could let Stan in on it, Mr. President? It would make my job a lot easier."

"I suppose you're right, but I've got a gut feeling about this, that it could make the development of the atomic bomb look like just another firecracker."

""Yes sir, I'm inclined to share your feeling," Felix said.

"Good. It's late now, but I'd like you to come back tomorrow morning at ten o'clock. No, make that eight o'clock. I want a complete briefing on everything you have."

"Yes, sir." Felix sensed his cue and stood up.

The President offered his hand again. "See you in the morning, then. Ask Ruth to put it into the calendar for then and reschedule what was there, would you please?"

"Yes, sir. Good night, Mr. President."

He shook hands with both of the Secretaries and left.

CHAPTER III

(38 HOURS EARLIER)

Eric Corbett pondered the emotions he would feel later if this greatest of all possible adventures that he was about to embark upon should fail. It was conceivable that he might still be around to read the note he had just written; or he could be God only knew where. The thought brought a smile to the corners of his mouth.

The note was addressed to Dr. Wendell Perry. Wendell was a long time friend and supporter who had, on more than one occasion, provided the brilliance that had shown the way out of an equation headed for certain failure back onto a path of renewed possibility.

Wendell was also his boss, although the word "boss" would scarcely be recognized in the vocabulary of the employees of this fecund world of intellectual misfits.

If one zoomed over the city in a low-flying helicopter they would see a carpet of factories, warehouses, hospitals, schools and a multitude of other places where bosses dwell. Bosses that hire, fire, give promotions, raises, reprimands or praise with regularity. Some people will do anything to gain their attention. Others will do anything to avoid it. But then, the bosses, like a lot of other things at this N.A.S.A. facility at Cal Tech, offered very little that conformed to the rest of the world. From their organizational structure, through their systems and procedures, right down to their mind boggling projects, this small wing, nearly lost on the huge campus, would surely stand out as unique to the helicopter passenger if they could somehow gain access to its interior, which they could not.

Since a "lack of need" had plunged the word boss into obscurity, Wendell was just Wendell to his friends and colleagues. For reasons important to the rest of the world, there was a personnel form in his filing cabinet that had a space next to the word TITLE into which someone had typed the words DEPARTMENT HEAD, not "manager," or "superintendent," but HEAD. Eric had known Wendell, on a few social occasions after his third glass of Chablis, to refer to himself as the HEAD HEAD. This is reference to his being overseer of one of our nation's most distinguished "Think Tanks," he would then inevitably chuckle at his own witticism. As for Eric, he never missed this opportunity to solicit Wendell's opinion as to why a grown man, whose I.Q. registered in the low ISO's, would have the sense of humor of a ten year old.

These kinds of unprovoked attacks from Eric served to remind Wendell what good friends they really were. After all, Eric wouldn't say something that rotten to somebody he didn't really like.

Actually, the two men did not have a great deal in common. Wendell was only ten years older than Eric, but Wendell had been fifty-seven all his life. Probably the strongest catalyst bonding their relationship was their mutual admiration for each other's mathematical skills. That, and their shared experience of growing up in a world where, despite every effort on their part to be just one of the guys, they both often made their peers and adults feel uncomfortable or inadequate in their presence.

Eric remembered being considered from childhood as one of those rare creatures that defy explanation as to their phyletic origin. He could recall his father saying "I could never add two and two, and he sure as hell didn't get it from his mother's side of the family!"

Somehow or other, the ability to learn and understand things was much easier for him than it was for other people.

The price one pays for this gift (or curse) begins in the formative years; when most children were into breaking their toys, Eric could be found disassembling and analyzing his. Through the years he learned to cope with the rigors of being 'different'. He had had to deal with reactions from others ranging from ridicule to envy. He was the "kiss ass" who would rather stick his nose into a book than between Doris Cunningham's boobs.

The truth is, Eric wasn't at all opposed to any part of Doris Cunningham's anatomy. It was just that one day when he mentioned to her that he was reading Plato she expressed surprise that anyone would write such a big book about Mickey Mouse's dog.

Like most of his breed, he eventually sought out and built his life around "freaks" of his own kind. The only minor distinction, he liked to remind himself, was that instead of a carnival sideshow tent, he performed in a top secret government think tank. Instead of having two heads or the skin of a reptile, one simply had to be what the world labeled a 'genius'. Safe and secure in a world of other freaks who, even while socializing in the lunch room, might speak of diffraction, polarization, alpha-decay, mesons or emission theories instead of last night's bowling score.

This was not snobbery on anyone's part. It's just that if you were a senior, somehow incorrectly assigned to a third grade class, you would go to almost any lengths to seek out someone who didn't want to play marbles.

It's true, Wendell wasn't very funny, but then Don Rickles probably couldn't help him with his equations either. Anyway, it was getting time to go.

The contents of the note he was leaving for Wendell was more philosophical than technical. They carried only an occasional reference to his project. They did, however, mention that his efforts to transmit matter through a space/time continuum reversal had been rewarded and that his entire library and data were in the file to be released to the Board for feasibility documentation.

The one regret Eric had was that he had been less than completely honest with his old friend about his intentions or even, for that matter, his progress. He felt especially guilty since Wendell had gone out on a limb and spearheaded a rather large budget request for him - a request that was practically void of any of the "show cause" documentation usually required on procurement requisitions of that size.

His only justification for his action was that if he had revealed his final equations to Wendell he, friend or not, would have had no choice but to inform the Committee. That would have resulted in months or even years of full support testing and endless experiments. No, there was something burning inside him; something that would not wait. Whatever the consequences, he was prepared to pick up the tab for his decision.

On several, occasions in 1955, Eric had conferred with Dr. Einstein when he was in residence at the University. Eric was only a student of twenty at the time, but he had become totally obsessed with the principal of relativity. He was particularly fascinated with the concept that there are no "nows" in the universe.

There are no "ups" or "downs" and matter is energy and energy is matter. Nearly all the Newtonian laws were shattered with the variations of velocity as it related to matter in these findings. The principal of space being simply a measurement of time, and vice versa, became all-consuming to him. He had dedicated the past twenty-five years of his life to questioning the logic that stated that time could only run in one direction, from the past to the future.

It was in the field of quantum mechanics that dealt with sub atomic particles that even Einstein failed to unravel, and divided the scientific world into two vastly different camps, even using different mathematics. It wasn't until the genius mind of Stephen Hawking's equations focusing on the immeasurable density of the sub-atomic particles at the edge of a black hole drawing in and devouring all matter in a constellation, thus creating a worm hole in the curvature of space, which was the beginning of the connection on the two theories of general relativity and quantum mechanics.

Three days ago, he had come to the end of nearly a quarter-century of research, most of which had been made possible by University grants until NASA took over funding his work in 1978.

The last three days had been spent in getting his affairs together. On a visit to his safety deposit box it had occurred to him that he really had very little to do that would fall under the category of "getting one's affairs in order." The question even crossed his mind whether a man's worth in life could be measured by how complicated his affairs were to administer after his death; not that he anticipated any such occurrence.

At forty-seven, Eric had never been married. He had come close about seven years ago but the relationship didn't survive the division of their mutual interests, and his work proved to be his ultimate mistress.

Dedicated as he was to his work, Eric somehow just didn't fit the profile for central casting's version of a scientific egghead. Standing well over six feet tall, he possessed a lean, muscular build that was due more to a gift of nature than it was to any fitness program. His square jaw and deep set steel blue eyes were topped off with a thick crop of salt and pepper hair. Years of weekends at the beach near Malibu had carved his face into the ruggedly handsome type one might expect to find on a cigarette billboard. He also had a keen sense of humor not usually associated with an IQ of 170.

In fact, Eric Corbett was what you might call a living study of contradictions. Most men of science who, while they might have their own religious convictions, for the most part still clung tightly to their radioactive carbon clocks and evolutionary fossils. Many of his colleagues managed, with empathic pompous smiles, to allow the "less enlightened" of the world to unquestionably accept the Bible version of creation if they could draw some comfort from it. After all, even most clergymen don't take the Genesis account seriously. But for Eric Corbett, school was still out. At least by this account, intelligence, intent and direction antedated this magnificently designed and orderly universe instead of evolution's mechanism of time, chance and circumstance.

The ultimate, he believed, of every scientific goal would be that the extreme, and seemingly insurmountable limit of scientific knowledge, would be reached with the attainment of perfect isomorphic representation. That is, it could be reached in a final, flawless concurrence of theory and natural process, so complete that every observed phenomenon could be explained with nothing left to ponder.

His serious questioning began somewhere in his student years when, like many young, brilliant students, he was frustrated by the unanswered questions and dead ends in the field of evolution. Most chose to accept, at least tentatively, the theories and probability factors currently being offered as facts by institutions of higher learning. Young Eric Corbett, however, found many of these answers no more satisfying than the bottom-line answer he had always received from theologians as to WHY God operated the way he did, in a manner that went so far beyond human understanding. Both science and theology seemed always to require the seeker to "have faith."

He could remember with remarkable clarity back to an age where most people's memories have become obscured by time. As if it were only yesterday he heard the screen door slam shut on the back porch as he scampered up the open wooden steps leading from the basement. Stepping lightly he made sure he skipped the third and seventh steps, because their squeaks would reveal his presence to his parents in the kitchen and abort his opportunity to listen from behind the cellar door to all of that neat grown-up talk that children find so fascinating when they feel that their presence is undetected.

He heard his mother welcome Reverend Schroder and offer him a piece of freshly baked pumpkin pie. There was the inevitable refusal with a regretful reference to his waistline. A second urging, however, proved to be too tempting for the Reverend, who succumbed to a generous slice of Mrs. Corbett's pie.

The compliments on her pie and other predictable small talk continues for awhile as Eric perched on the step silently running a fingernail over the corduroy material of his knickers while his other hand fiddled with the laces of his gym shoes. Even though he didn't know what a premonition was, he somehow knew that the conversation would eventually get around to him. At the proper time (a concept understood only by adults), Reverend Schroder at last broached the subject of Eric.

"Mr. and Mrs. Corbett, I'd like to speak to you about Eric."

"What is it?" He remembered the concern in his mother's voice. "Has he done something wrong?"

"No, no. It's nothing like that. Eric is a fine boy. It's just that...well, it's a little hard to explain, but for want of a better way of putting it, I'll say Eric has been a bit disruptive in his Sunday school class."

"Disruptive?" Eric's father asked. "has he been acting up?"

"Well now, Mr. Corbett, not in a way you might expect. Heaven only knows we get enough of that from the other young boys. The problem, it seems, is the constant state of turmoil in which he keeps Miss Higgins and the rest of the class with his never-ending flow of questions. Some of them are downright unhealthy questions, I might add."

"Did Miss Higgins tell you what kind of questions, Reverend?" His father asked.

"Well, she said they usually deal with the sort of things a child his age shouldn't be concerned about. Things like, where did God come from and why do people have different gods? Silly questions like that. She said that in last Sunday's class he even asked her if Adam and Eve were created by God and weren't born like the rest of us, did they have belly buttons? Now really, Mr. Corbett, what kind of question is that?"

There were a few seconds of silence. Eric remembered sitting there behind the door, feeling a sense of guilt, knowing that he must have done something wrong, but not quite sure what his crime was. Finally he heard his father speak in his slow, deliberate manner.

"Well now, Reverend Schroder, I'm not sure what kind of a question it is for a six-year-old to ask, but I have to confess that in my thirty-three years, it's one I never thought of."

Eric recalled being very pleased with his father's answer. Most of the rest of the memory of Reverend Schroder's visit remained locked away in the archives of gray matter where, theoretically, every occurrence in one's lifetime is stored. There was some vague recollection of his parents assuring the Pastor that they would speak to Eric and instruct him to refrain from questioning Miss Higgins when the class was in session. "Faith would work wonders when evidence is not at hand," he recalled the Reverend's parting words.

Now here in his adult world he still regretfully found that faith was a commodity he possessed very little of. That was why, a year or so ago, he had decided to seek out this entity called God. With study and reasoning he hoped to minimize the need for faith or, if his efforts bore no fruit, perhaps he could then rest content with the idea that it was indeed man who created God, instead of the other way around. The second law of thermodynamics says that all systems tend toward the state of greater probability. He thus held that all the wonders of evolution could not have come about without the guidance of some form of intelligence.

He could conceive of no acceptable order of things that did not include a guiding force that preceded all other forms of matter that occupies space in the universe. So what is so unscientific about calling this intelligence "God," He thought. "After all, it's a short word and all encompassing. But if God really does exist, do we know anything about Him, Her, or It? Is it even necessary to know? Has a record been left?

One characteristic of human nature that he found objectionable was the practice of mimicry, an idiosyncrasy that plagued mankind in epidemic proportions. A staunch Democratic home usually produced offspring that represented future votes for that party line. Klansmen bred klansmen; Catholics, Catholics; Jews, Jews, and so it went.

Social environment and traditional inheritance far outweighed the occasional nonconformist who considered, at least, the possibility of a different path.

Simply being born into western civilization where Christianity was the predominant religion was not sufficient reason for him not to seek out answers in other major religions. In his initial probes, however, he determined that they all seemed to deal more with philosophy than with attempting to provide answers about the origin of anything. Making no judgments about the credibility of the balance of the book he liked, at least, the first three words he found in the Bible, "In the beginning," now that, he thought, makes a statement. Although he found, as he began exploring this book further, that he was almost immediately confronted by a deluge of statements that fell well outside the boundaries of his existing belief system.

It began like an adult fairytale, and he recalled asking himself at times how anyone could expect even a child to believe such tripe. He struggled through the accounts of creation that were made incredible by the time spans allotted to various incidents that were said to have occurred. Fortunately, he dragged up from somewhere back in his memory a statement he recalled being made by Dr. Einstein: "'Common sense' is merely an accumulation of prejudices, laid down prior to the age of sixteen." It helped him keep an open mind.

Wrestling his way through the archaic laws of Leviticus and Deuteronomy was tedious and pure drudgery. Eric had never found the acquisition of knowledge to be so dull. But perseverance prevailed, and eventually a pattern of credibility began to emerge. Yet, after the first complete reading there still appeared to be more contradictions than he considered acceptable.

Perhaps the thing that fascinated him the most and inspired him to continue his study was the way the Old and New Testaments tied together but were meaningless and unsubstantiated apart from each other.

Another area that intrigued him was the fact that this one book, divided into two parts, was really sixty-six books written over a period of sixteen hundred years by thirty-five or more authors. The authors could not have known each other, yet they tied together a chain of events which included a fulfillment of prophecy that could not have possibly happened simply by chance. His mathematical mind could have stretched the odds to allow for ten, or even twenty, predictions coming to pass (especially if the one fulfilling the prophecy had knowledge of its expectations). But in his research he had recorded over a hundred references and prophecies in the Old Testament that became fulfilled in the New. So many occurrences removed any doubt that Jesus was the One made reference to by the prophets in the Hebrew scriptures. The last of these prophets died at least six hundred years prior to the arrival of Jesus, who was born at the exact time, in the exact place, and from the proper ancestry (the line of David). These were hardly controllable incidents for an unborn child.

The Book said he was not born of man, but that God placed the seed into a virgin so that he would be born without sin. The purpose of his coming, it stated, was to establish a new covenant with man in that he came not to replace the law but, rather, to fulfill it. He was to be offered as a sacrifice on behalf of mankind, to remove the sins that all had inherited from Adam and Eve.

This original pair, the scriptures stated, did not evolve but were created by God in a perfect, sinless condition.

Much of it made nice reading, with its promise of the abolition of evil and suffering, along with a resurrection that offered that opportunity of gaining everlasting life. But... WOW! What about all the suffering He allowed, and the killing of people He sanctioned? Was all of this really to be believed without an extraordinary amount of that illusive ingredient called faith?

The single question that kept recurring to Eric was the same one that Pontius Pilate asked of Jesus, "what is truth?" In his mind, this commingled with the question, "Was it accidental evolution, without intent or purpose, or was it creation that included both?" There were times when he hated the limitations of his mind that could not expand to the concept of a supreme being who created by simply willing something to be...creation without instrumentation... inconceivable. But still, how much more conceivable than the probability of a single cell constructing and giving life to itself.

There were other times when he considered what he referred to as the "great scam" theory. Could it be that all books dealing with gods and religion served in the past as a means for men of letters to gain power over the vast uneducated populous; power gained by declaring that these were not their words, but the words of the gods? That to disobey them would not only bring punishment, but also deprive them of their rewards. That their only salvation was to place their minds, souls and tithings into the hand of the priests. A place called Jonestown was a good example of the power of this kind of mind control, even in a literate world.

It was a constant struggle for him to keep setting aside his prejudices. He would be reading a passage when suddenly some wall would shoot up and an inner voice would say, "Naa!" They've got to be kidding. How could that be?"

Every once in a while a piece of trivia that had little to do with the story would spring up to re-ignite his interest. One was the reference to the world as a circle or globe, although the Earth was to be considered flat for millenniums to come.

Another passage stated that the rabbit was a "cud chewing animal." He recalled reading an article in one of his journals that said researchers were surprised to discover that the rabbit was a cud chewing animal - in 1947! How could the writers of the Bible have known of these things so many years ago?

This sort of trivia would hardly be the inspiration for most people to continue their efforts, but to Eric it gave credibility to a story where it was much needed.

Soon learning to use the specialized reference books, he became aware that the passages in the Bible were constantly referring to different times in history. Similarly, he hoped it would be possible for some as yet unwritten equation to be scribbled on a blackboard and allow an object on this planet to be placed in a time slot that history considers already to have happened.

In what he referred to as the "pit stops" of concentration, those pauses which every scholar must make from time to time in order to keep their brains from exploding, he often escaped to fantasy. One of his favorite fantasies was placing himself in the same room with Dr. Einstein and sharing in the elation of writing the equation $E=mc$. He could imagine the unequaled ecstasy one would surely feel when this brilliant mind finally arrived, after thousands of prior equations, at the value of the equivalent mass of energy. How Eric's heart would have pounded as he took the simple remaining step and wrote on the board the most important and famous equation in history: $E=mc^2$.

Back to reality, as he devoted more time to his study of the Bible he gradually found that he was able to lay aside more of the objections that had once caused him to reject many of the statements in the Book. Still, there was one area of concern that conflicted so violently with the things he presently believed that he felt he might never resolve it. That had to do with the chronological dates the Bible placed on events and the longevity of people prior to the deluge of Noah's time. He couldn't imagine those things to be accurate, since they were inconsistent with both modern medicine and our present technology for measuring the age of objects by carbon count.

This was a hurdle he would have to overcome in order to be able to proceed with his studies and still not totally discard the training and logic that were so much a part of him. With limited knowledge of this field, he approached the dilemma in typical Corbett style.

First, he emptied himself of any preconceived ideas he might have regarding fact versus theory. Then he buried

33

himself in the campus library to absorb and decipher all the information he could lay his hands on.

Six days later his conclusions were still not black or white, but he had produced enough gray area that he could now feel comfortable with many of those Biblical time spans that he had once considered to be in irreconcilable conflict with the world of science.

His findings could not be condensed to a few words, but in lieu of no explanation at all, he would have offered the following summation to any inquisitive colleague unfortunate enough to have asked:

In accepting the accuracy of the carbon dating method the first thing one has to do is make certain assumptions -

(I) Carbon-I4, the radioactive component of natural carbon, decays at the rate of a half life of 5,568 years, and,

(2) The ratio of carbon-I4 atoms to the stable carbon-I2 atoms in live carbon has always been the same as it is today. These two assumptions are dependent on two others -

(I) The number of carbon-I4 atoms has remained constant, with no variation of the cosmic rays that formed them over the past I5,000 to 20,000 years, and,

(II) The total amount of stable carbon in the exchange reservoir has remained constant and not contaminated by carbon dioxide in the air or other living things.

If any of these assumptions breaks down the entire method breaks down and will not give the correct date.

The first samples of wood tested from Egyptian tombs gave reasonably acceptable accuracy to a determinable date in history of approximately 4,000 years ago. However, the discrepancies due to variations of conditions and testing methods were horrendous.

The absolute calibration of the gas counter, which determines the specific disintegration rate for the subsequent mass of spectrographic measurement of the exact quantity of C-I4, was extremely variable due to absorption into the walls of the container in the introduction process.

Changes in the Earth's magnetic field and solar phenomena also cause great fluctuations in cosmic rays reaching the Earth. Another contributor to inconsistencies in this method of dating are the cataclysmic changes that have taken place in the Earth's atmospheric and surface conditions as a result of global deluge.

If the Biblical account of the deluge and the existing shroud, or water canopy that surrounded the Earth was true, it would indeed offer an explanation to many perplexing questions surrounding the carbon dating methods.

The water shroud also would have provided the Biblical Adam with the perfect tropical greenhouse conditions for his paradise garden, and a constant temperature for his naked comfort.

The oceans, too, must have become much greater in expanse and depth after the flood, as the weight of the water pushed the plastic mantle away from the ocean bed towards the continents, pushing up gigantic new mountains. This would ultimately have given the oceans a much larger capacity to carry dissolved carbonation. Simultaneously, the removal of the shield allowed for the admission of enormous amounts of solar rays, thereby increasing the rate of production of carbon-14.

The reality of a world wide flood was confirmed by the presence of sea life fossils in all parts of the globe, including the tops of the highest mountains. He wondered, too, if the catastrophic changes that must have taken place at that time might not explain the discovery of bison in the polar regions, their flesh still intact, but frozen so quickly while they grazed that one of the animals still had a buttercup in its mouth.

The pitfalls due to the range of variation possible in tree ring counting, used in calibrating the radio carbon clock, along with all the other allowable adjustments incorporated in the dating process, caused Eric to conclude that there was literally more "faith" required to accept the infallibility of this dating method than was required to accept the Biblical report of a deluge some 4,350 years ago.

There was also heavily documented evidence of the ark, or at least portions of it, still in existence on the ever-shifting crevasses of Mount Ararat.

There were, then, two contributing factors to this time dilemma that had concerned him so much. For one, the dating of objects would be greatly affected by whether they had occurred before or after the flood. The other was the decline from the state of perfection that marked Adam's beginning. He recalled, at one point, a statement in the Book that said, "A day to God is as a thousand years." Was there a connection, then, when God told Adam that if he ate of a certain fruit that on that day he would surely die?

Adam lived to be 930 years old. Noah, a close descendent of Adam's, lived to be 950 years old. However, after the flood there was a rapid decline in the recorded life spans of man, and it soon became the same as today's life expectancy.

Not white, but no longer black, a gray area of possibility now existed wherein the Bible and science were no longer necessarily deadlocked in an irreconcilable impasse. Somehow in his mind he had suddenly flattened out that last hurdle of skepticism. While still not able to cry, "Yes, Lord, now I believe," he no longer felt the denial of credibility he once felt for the Scriptures.

Now his quest for verification took on an even greater urgency.

Ever since receiving the original grant, thirteen years and three renewals ago, Eric had been visited by only two Congressional Committees. The last four members to be escorted by Wendell were checking into things in a rather routine way. This was fine with Eric, who preferred to keep a low profile with his project. He diplomatically employed the old axiom that if you can't impress them with the credibility of your project, dazzle them with bullshit.

There was a better than ever chance that these respected members of Congress differed little from the Budget Committee or even from the other staff members at this facility; they considered his efforts interesting but short on feasibility. The only other research reported being done on gyro-time manipulation was in Budapest. As yet, there had been no information exchange program worked out with the Soviet Scientific Exchange Commission.

The lower the profile, the less interference from the various steering committees. Eric was certain that the Hungarian project was the only justification NASA needed to keep his work from falling victim to the ever-honoring ax. He knew that the Committee had little or no faith that his self-contained gyro capsule, with its banks of yet to be programmed computers, would even transport a speck of sand back into the moment of time that had just passed, let alone fourteen hundred pounds (one of the constants in all his equations) back two thousand years.

His procedural manual called for the usual policy of witnessed documentation of all progressive experiments. One, in its final stages, even called for the placement and return of a mini-camera and recorder at Pearl Harbor on December 7th, 1941.

He agreed with the Committee on at least this one point: this was an experiment that would never take place. The normal processes of scientific endeavor; requiring years of research to isolate a virus strain or develop a rocket fuel simply did not apply to his project. No gray area here. His calculations were either correct or they weren't. Nor was there any time for procedural matters. There was something he had to know - now. Blessed are those who can say, "God, I know you're there," he thought, instead of a jerk like me who says, "God, I think you're there but I'll know for sure just as soon as we've had a little chat."

CHAPTER IV

It was one of those misty nights that Californians refuse to call rain but which nevertheless require the use of windshield wipers. The streets and trees next to the streetlamps glittered as Eric drove his car through the campus and pulled into the parking lot of the Research Center. He pulled into his assigned space, turned off the engine, and started to remove his keys from the ignition. He hesitated for an instant, shrugged, and left the keys where they were. He grabbed the small bag off the seat next to him and walked into the building. In the lobby he was greeted by one of the three security guards, (a condition that would appear to the casual observer to be a classic example of government feather bedding).

"Evening, Mr. Corbett, I haven't seen you since I came off day shift."

"How've ya been, Ralph?"

"Fine, thank you, sir. Going to burn a little midnight oil?"

"Yeah, you know how it is. We sit here all day long and stare at the wall, then right in the middle of the late show what we've been trying to think of all day suddenly comes to us."

"So that's the way it works! I always wondered how you people came up with your ideas."

"Now you know. They're all inspired by T.V."

"Yes, sir. May I see what's in the bag, sir?"

"Sure." Eric handed him the tote bag.

Ralph's face registered confusion as he pulled out some robes and sandals, along with a hand-sewn water bag, a pouch of old coins, and some other strange items. He looked at Eric and didn't have to say a word.

"Oh, that stuff," Eric smiled. "It's a costume Doreen made for a Halloween party we've been invited to. We thought we'd just dress and go from here to save a little time."

Eric knew that most of the employees in the building had seen he and Doreen together enough at coffee breaks and other occasions that guards would have no problem with his explanation. Lies never set well with him especially since Doreen knew nothing of the contents of the bag or their intended use but the situation demanded it.

"I see." Ralph accepted the explanation. "So you're going as a monk or something, huh?"

"Something like that."

Ralph replaced the items and they walked over to the scanner. Eric placed his hand on it, they both inserted their cards, and the door opened.

"Have a nice night, sir," Ralph said, handing him the bag.

"I'm sure going to try, Ralph," Eric smiled.

He walked down the corridor, unlocked his door and entered his lab. When he switched on the light his eyes followed along an entire wall lined with panels of instruments and came to rest upon the object in the center of the room. It resembled a cylindrical shower curtain attached to tracks at the floor and ceiling. There was the usual desk, filing cabinets, and the inevitable large chalkboard that bore traces of erased equations.

Eric laid his bag on the desk and went over to a filing cabinet, which he unlocked. He removed a single sheet of paper and then turned on the computer, causing several instruments on the panel to come to life. He made several entries, the last of which read "ROTATIONS: 19,761,211,000." Then he paused with his finger over a key as he watched a digital counter spinning seconds, tenths of seconds and hundredths of seconds. Suddenly he pushed the key and said aloud, "Mark!"

Another panel contained a clock reading five minutes and counting down. His face registered the look of a pilot who has just committed himself to the point of no return.

He walked over to the curtain, unlocked it and pushed it open. Inside was a dome-shaped capsule of Plexiglas suspended in air by small horizontal cables attached to an outer ring of steel. Above and below were flat circular rings with no moving parts, save a small bead of light rotating slowly within a narrow strip of glass around the circumference of the rings. The top and bottom rotated in different directions. The capsule contained a single seat and a control panel.

He took a deep breath and walked over to the desk and started to unpack his tote bag. His heart nearly jumped into his mouth when there was a knock at the door, and he frantically shoved the contents back into the bag. Before he was composed enough to respond, Doreen Schuler opened the door which he had carelessly left unlocked.

"Eric, what in the world are you doing here? Are they paying you by the hour now?" Doreen was a pretty, thirty-five year old microbiologist who worked in the lab across the hall.

"Oh, ah, no. No. I just ah... I just had an equation bouncing around in my head and I wanted to see how it would fly on the computer."

"Are you O.K.?" She asked.

"I'm fine... Fine, just a little busy at the moment."

"Wow," she said, looking at the panel, "you've got the whole Christmas tree lit up tonight. You must have entered a whole new program." She started to enter the room but Eric walked over to head her off.

"No," he said, taking her arm, "just doing some dry run testing."

"Eric," she said, "I know what you're doing is Top Secret, but what you're working on is no secret. Did that make sense?"

"In its own way."

"I mean. I know what you're working on has to do with time manipulation, or something like that. But do you really believe that sort of thing can be done?"

"I don't know, Doreen, I really don't know. But right now you'll have to excuse me. I do have some things on a countdown I have to get back to."

"Oh, hey, I'm sorry. I didn't mean to barge in. I was just surprised to see your light on."

"No problem. I'll see you later," he said, ushering her out.

"Sure," she said. "I've got some cultures in the oven that need tending anyway. Listen, just in case you get bored watching the lights flash, would you consider letting a lady buy you a nightcap at this little after hours dump she knows?"

"I tell you what. This particular night is a little up in the air, but can I have a rain check on that?"

"Anytime." She smiled, and left the room.

Eric turned and hurried back to his desk, glancing at the digital clock, which now read three minutes. He hurriedly undressed and got into the robe and sandals.

He checked and double-checked all systems and the list of items that were to make the journey with him. Then he neatly placed them all back into the hand-sewn goatskin backpack he had labored over so tediously in the kitchen of his studio apartment. He placed the pack into the compartment under the capsule's single control seat. Most of the items in the pack were miniaturized, so the entire inventory weighed less than thirty-seven pounds.

He could not be certain where the capsule would stabilize geographically. This was by far the most difficult area to program of all of his computations. In nearly two thousand years of orbiting the Sun, the Earth would have rotated on its axis over nineteen and a half billion miles.

His destination was Jerusalem, and he hoped to stabilize between the years 30 to 33 A. D. of our calendar, although most scholars, allowing for adjustments in the Julian and Gregorian calendars, put the birth of Jesus closer to the year 6 A.D. To end his journey within sight of the city would be like dropping a golf ball into a tin cup from the top of a twenty story building. It was imperative that he come to rest

41

on land in the Eastern hemisphere. If he miscalculated and ended up in the New World there would be no way to reach what we now know as the Middle East; he would spend his time in the wilderness of a land that no white man had ever seen at that time.

Any land, however, would be preferable to the 75% of the globe covered by water - a calculated risk he tried not to think about.

Less than two minutes left now.

He began to be aware of his heart pounding faster. God, how many years had he dreamed of this moment! First things, first, he kept telling himself. After all, if he didn't arrive at his destination none of the other details would be of any consequence anyway.

It was imperative that he blend into the environment, that no one even suspect he was anything but a traveling merchant. Eric knew very well from his studies that the people of that period were superstitious, that they were believers in omens and subjected to many men who called themselves the "Messiah." The nation was seething in political, religious, and economic unrest. In order to remain unmolested in his journey to seek out Jesus he must remain unnoticed. One of the most commonly displayed characteristics of mankind was that people feared that which they did not understand - a characteristic which, unfortunately, the centuries have done little to change.

He threw the final switch. He was fully on computer now. As he lowered himself into the control chair to watch the countdown he felt an inexplicable flow of contentment surge through his body. This was something he had not expected. His expectation had been for a massive flow of adrenalin, causing any number of anxieties. What he was feeling instead he really counted as a blessing, and he was grateful.

There was less than a minute to go now. His eyes left the digital counter and glanced down at the clothing he had fashioned for himself. Although he had hand-sewn his rough sandals and robes he wondered if the machine-woven material would be detected by anyone. A little bit late to be worrying about that sort of thing, he thought.

Less than forty seconds left. He started to practice various words in Hebrew, Greek, Aramaic and Latin. Although he had mastered all four languages he could only guess at their pronunciation; the centuries would have changed their sound and meaning to some extent. However, his mind soon wandered from this exercise and he found himself in prayer.

"Dear God," he said aloud, "I recall your Son's statement to Thomas, that blessed are those who do not see and yet believe. I pray to you, Father, that you do not look with displeasure upon my attempts to make this journey to contact your Son, so that I might see. I know that you caused to be written that the wisdom of man is but foolishness to God, but if..." Zero! It had begun!

He could only hear a slight hum at first, as the powerful gyros began to create a counter-electromagnetic field. The only physical sensation was a feeling that his body was growing heavier. This was not, however, the same sensation experienced in the G forces of acceleration, it was more like his body was being impacted equally from all directions. The noise increased to a deafening pitch, and his body continued to feel like it was increasing in density. Only seconds before it happened he felt the blackout coming over him.

Once again there was a knock at the door. This time Doreen waited before knocking again and entering.

"Eric, I'm sorry, but I forgot to..." she stopped. One of those intuitions often attributed to women told her that something was wrong.

"Eric," she called again. "Are you here?"

No answer. She stood there, her eyes scanning the silent room. Then her gaze focused upon the empty area within the curtain. She approached slowly and stood in front of it. Instinctively she reached out her hand as if to verify her sense of sight with that of touch. As her hand passed into the space her fingers disappeared. She jerked her hand back, too frightened to scream. She examined her hand. It was intact;

there was no effect. She watched in awe as the smoke from her cigarette drifted into the empty area and disappeared abruptly. Slowly again she put her hand back into the area, watching it disappear well past her wrist before withdrawing it. She paused, dumbfounded. She took a pen from the pocket of her lab coat and threw it into the blank space. It disappeared for about three feet, then reappeared and fell to the floor on the other side of nothing. There was a hole in the universe that nothing could exist in...because it wasn't there. Doreen could only whisper, "Oh my God!"

CHAPTER V

His eyes opened slowly and he sat motionless, almost afraid to move as he scanned the barren landscape outside the capsule window. There was not a sound to be heard as he stared in silence, attempting to collect his thoughts.

"I've done it!" He screamed aloud, breaking the silence and startling himself with the sound of his own voice. "I don't know where I am or what time or date it is, but I'm sure as hell not in Pasadena, California." He was drowning in his own excitement, but forced himself to sit quietly and regain his composure.

He finally moved his hand to the instrument panel and touched a single button, which shut down the power unit. There was absolute silence. He reached down and threw the latch, allowing himself to open the thin windowed door of the capsule and step out onto the rocky desert floor.

The temperature was pleasant, somewhere in the low 80's, and there was just a slight breeze blowing. He guessed it to be mid-morning, but a time fix would have to wait until later.

Standing upright, scanning a 360 degree view of the landscape, what he saw was what he expected the wilderness of the Middle East to look like. However, he could be in Utah or Australia for all he knew. As he stood gazing at the horizons he was once again aware of a change in his body. He examined his hands and felt different parts of his anatomy, but his brief examination turned up nothing unusual.

He decided to examine the terrain more closely, and walked over to some small boulders next to a dry stream bed. Picking up a few, he quickly determined that they were granite, as he fondled them briefly in his hand. Then, putting a slight bit of pressure on one of the rocks with his thumb, he jumped a little with surprise as the rock disintegrated.

He began to examine the fragments. He was no geology major, but he was sure he knew the difference between granite and sandstone. For the life of him, the rocks appeared to be solid granite. The only difference was that they seemed very light in weight, but he could not explain the reason for their crumbling under such minor pressure.

He examined another rock, letting it fall several times on a larger boulder that was obviously solid granite. The smaller rock bounced off the larger boulder with the clear, sharp impact he expected, and it remained intact as it fell to the desert floor. Eric picked up the stone and squeezed it quite gently in his hand. His brow drew into a questioning frown as he felt the rock crumbling and radiating warmth in the palm of his hand. He stood there for a while, searching for an explanation, but came up empty.

Feeling frustrated, and not really knowing why he did it, he walked over to a larger boulder partially embedded in the ground a few feet away. Prepared for a struggle in dislodging and lifting the larger stone, he was met with yet another surprise as he lifted it effortlessly out of its resting place. It seemed to weigh no more than a baseball.

He stared in amazement at the boulder, which he estimated to weigh forty or fifty pounds. He again acted without knowing why, throwing the boulder out into the desert, and then stood dumbfounded, as he watched the stone sail through the air about two hundred yards. It landed on the desert floor in a heavy impact of dust and flying gravel. "What in hell..." Eric said aloud, but didn't finish the sentence. He could only stand in wonderment as he watched the dust settle in the distance where the boulder had landed.

Eventually, with a shake of his head, he reminded himself that he was a scientist and that there had to be a reasonable explanation for what he had just witnessed. No one could throw a baseball that far, let alone a fifty-pound boulder! It was as though the gravitational field had somehow been affected, but that made no sense at all.

Then a thought occurred to him, and he ran back to the capsule. Reaching under the seat, he pulled out the goatskin backpack. He knew that it weighed just under thirty-seven pounds. Lifting the pack confirmed that it was heavy and probably did, indeed, weigh the same as it had before. He put the pack down and walked over to a huge boulder weighing probably two tons. He shoved it, and was again amazed to see the boulder move a few inches.

There could only be one explanation. The capsule and the objects in it, including himself, were subjected to velocity fields of nearly twice the speed of light. Einstein stated that as matter neared light-speed velocity it would increase in mass. He was the same size, relative to the objects around him, but somehow there must have been a tremendous increase in his density. That increase resulted in other objects weighing far less to him. In other words, he had become capable of performing superhuman feats of strength.

After contemplating this new and unexpected development for several minutes he realized that it was distracting him from the truly important things he should be doing. He needed to find out where he was, and when. This, of course, meant beginning his journey and making contact with people, if there were any to be found.

Using his newly developed ability, he proceeded to hide his capsule by encasing it with huge, "feather weight" boulders. After making a few notes and drawings about its location, he gathered up the backpack and headed out in a northerly direction, without having the slightest idea why he chose that course. Yeah, he did... that's the way his compass pointed.

He walked for over two hours without so much as a sign that other life even existed on this planet. The position of the sun indicated that it was mid-afternoon. Finding a rock ledge he could sit under, he consumed some squeeze tube nourishment, and drank some water. He resented the fact that eight pounds of his backpack was due to man's inability to miniaturize, compress, or develop a substitute for water.

He scanned the horizon for some sign of civilization, but the barren landscape yielded no clues. Some of the initial excitement of accomplishment was giving way to his impatience to verify his position in time and geography. The desolate wilderness was also giving rise to some concern; he wondered if he would ever locate other human beings.

Setting off again, he used his compass to maintain a straight line and eliminate needless circling or deviations. He had been walking for over two hours since his last break, and the sun was probably half an hour away from setting. It was time to start looking for a suitable place to spend the night. He changed course slightly to parallel the foothills, knowing this would be the most likely area to find water.

Suddenly he spotted something that made his pulse beat a little faster. There appeared to be an area on one of the hills ahead of him with an unnaturally flat surface running across it. He started walking a little faster, sometimes nearly running, in the direction of the flat area in order to examine it more closely.

As he neared the site he noticed other areas that did not appear to be natural formations. His excitement grew and his pace quickened until he finally arrived and was standing on the spot. It confirmed what he had been hoping for. Eric was standing on a man-made road!

He exploded with a thunderous whoop of excitement, not caring that the rocks and mountains were his only audience. Now he knew that someone else existed, and had labored on this road. It was actually not much more than a crude dirt trail but it obviously led somewhere; it was the path to civilization. At least now he had something to follow.

The major decision he now had to make was which direction to follow the road, but this was a decision he had no intention of making until tomorrow, when he would be rested. Before him stretched a long night in which to ponder and record some of the activities of this most momentous of all days, that had really begun less than eight hours ago.

He found a small cave to settle into for his first night. It wasn't big enough to stand up in, but it was adequate for a night's lodging. To add to his already brightened spirits he discovered that the cave was inhabited by a small lizard who quickly yielded possession to the unwelcome intruder. All day long he hadn't seen so much as an insect or a shrub, but now he was assured that life existed and, thus, that survival was possible.

In a climate of joy, excitement, apprehension, contentment, and perhaps a dozen other mixed emotions he made his camp. From his pack he pulled out a strange combination of the goatskin bed roll and primitive water bag that were meant for the eyes of a beholder in the first century A.D., and instruments of such advanced technology that most people of the twentieth century would find them awesome. This miniaturized hardware, that would have been the envy of a producer of James Bond movies, would have to be guarded closely in order for him to travel unnoticed on his journey in search of this controversial carpenter from Nazareth. After rolling out his blankets he took two small capsules and a swallow of water. They gave him the fulfillment of a six-course meal, but not the satisfaction.

The sun had nearly set as he took two small instruments from his bag. One was a solar rechargeable lamp. It could focus into a beam, or illuminate an area with the lumen power of a 500 watt bulb on full power. The other was a small recorder, which he would use to document his journey.

He recorded for some time. He did his best to remain scientific but the emotions of the evening made it difficult not to ramble onto philosophical side paths. The light was, of course, not necessary, but somehow it eased the terrible aloneness he was feeling. In spite of the montage of thoughts racing through his mind exhaustion from the energy expended on the day's events finally superseded all other things, and he fell into a deep sleep. He slept surprisingly well, awakened only once by a noise. Briefly beaming the light across the landscape outside the cave he saw nothing, and almost immediately fell back to sleep again.

As the first rays of the morning sun entered the tiny cave Eric woke with a start, to find that he had to deal with a startling development.

Not ten feet away, kneeling down and staring into the cave at him, was a bearded man dressed in a hooded robe and sandals.

A third party observer would have been hard put to decide which of the two men was more surprised as they stared at one another. They resembled chimpanzees having their first encounter with a mirror.

For Eric, the passing seconds were agony. He wanted to shout a hundred questions at the man but he knew he must get him to speak first in order to determine the language, if he could. He forced away his stare of wonderment and gave a smiling nod toward the stranger, hoping for a verbal greeting in return.

The gesture worked. The man spoke to Eric in what he was sure was Aramaic, but was not any common greeting he had learned. The words sounded like, "Are you him?" Still not confident enough to speak, Eric gave the man a quizzical expression and grunted an omni lingual "Huh?" This time there was no doubt that the man was speaking Aramaic, as he rephrased his words which were a question, not a greeting.

"Are you the one we were told was coming?"

In his joy Eric rose so fast he hit his head on the rock ceiling of the cave, but felt no pain. He wanted to grab the stranger and dance. Dear God, the man's speaking Aramaic. He had made it! He was somewhere in Palestine! The celebration would have to wait. Right now he must concern himself with the problem at hand.

Not quite knowing how to deal with the question, Eric parried with questions. "Why do you ask me this?" and "Who is it you are expecting?"

"Last night I was camped near here and I noticed this strange light coming out of the hillside. I approached your camp silently to explore this mystery and I observed you sitting beside this box that gave off light but yet had no flame, and you were speaking in tongues to yet another box you held in your hand. During the night as I slept I accidentally kicked a rock which awakened us both. I then saw you search for the source of the sound with a line of light that came out of your hand and lit up the desert floor in its path."

Eric said nothing, and the man continued.

"My name is Ishmael, son of Jedakiah, and I am studying to become a scribe at Kahalpia, near Edh Dhanriye. The things I saw were not of man and so I say to you, 'Are you him? The one who is expected, and will free us from the Romans?'"

"My name is Eric. I am a stranger in your land, but I am only a traveling merchant, not the person you speak of. The things you saw were nothing more than new contraptions from Egypt that I intend to market in Persia and throughout Palestine. I would ask you not to mention them to others, lest I lose my marketing advantage. In return for your silence I will give you a personal demonstration of their workings."

He seemed to accept this, at least for the moment. "I am anxious to learn more about your country. Would you mind if I traveled with you for a way?" Eric said, hoping to turn the subject away from the light.

Ishmael was delighted with the request and consented so eagerly that Eric felt it was going to be a game of "who is going to get their questions in first."

Both men gathered their things and started walking, with Eric being sure to let Ishmael lead the way. It never occurred to Ishmael that the mysterious stranger would be heading in any direction other than towards Beersheba, having come from Egypt.

Eric wondered if it was not the custom to start the day off with a morning meal. He was starving, but he dare not consume a capsule, which would only lead to further questions. Still, if presented the offer, he would probably sell his soul for a cup of coffee.

Without Eric's persuasion, Ishmael began volunteering information about himself. The third son of modestly wealthy parents, his father was an importer, mostly of oils and fibers, in Casearea and thus he understood somewhat the necessity of trade secrets. Although for the life of him, he could not recall his father ever mentioning any products as wondrous as these from Egypt.

His two older brothers had both married and joined his father in business, but he had no mind for it, and he requested permission from his father, who himself was a Pharisee, to pursue a life in the priesthood. As a scribe he could not be ordained until he reached thirty; then he could be addressed as Rabbi.

Now he was only an apprentice scribe whose job was to count the number of letters on every line of scripture being transcribed from one scroll to the newly formed papyrus sheet that would become a new scroll. This count would be verified by no less than three apprentices, one scribe and one overseer to insure that it was an exact duplicate, in every detail, to the scrolls from which it was copied. This was the care taken to insure accuracy in perpetuation of the written word. The scribe would submit the scroll for verification upon completion of each quarter of the work. Since the slightest deviation from the original meant that the entire scroll must be removed and prepared for storage one hoped that if an error was detected it would not occur in the third or final quarter.

Another of Ishmael's duties was to scorch the ends of defective scrolls and place them in clay containers, which he stored in a small room. Every third month, these would be hauled away on an ass by two priests who took them off to be hidden in a secret cave in the desert known only to the hierarchy of the priesthood. The scrolls could not be destroyed because they had too closely approached a state of holiness to simply be discarded in the lime pits.

Ishmael carried on for some time about his duties. He was a pleasant and obviously dedicated young man in his early twenties. Eric guessed that a short but muscular physique was hidden under his heavily woven robe, fringed at the corners with long tassels. He was trying desperately to grow a beard but, alas, the thinly connected clumps of hair on his face fairly cried out for someone to shave them off in hopes that he could make a better start in another year or two.

As his enthusiastic young traveling companion continued with the disruptive details of his duties, he soon became engrossed with issues of a more political nature. Eric appreciated his insight, even though it was only the opinion of one man. It was like reading history out of a two thousand-year old manuscript. For his part, Ishmael just seemed grateful to have a willing ear at his disposal. He described his resentment of the Sadducees, a group consisting of rich, influential descendents of ruling families along with the scribes, priests, elders, and even the high priests, who made up the Sanhedrin, the seventy-one member judicial body governing Jewish law. As a Pharisee, Ishmael's dissatisfaction was focused on their policy of cooperation with Rome, which he saw as a compromise intended to preserve their own authority. Even Caiaphas, the High Priest who presided over their proceedings, wasn't excluded from this judgment.

From his study of history Eric knew that it was this division between the Pharisees and the Sadducees, sparked by the rebellious Zealots, that would, thirty or forty years hence, lead to a revolt against Rome that would result in the crushing destruction of Jerusalem and the Jewish nation.

Still, for the present, he was ecstatic about his good fortune to not only have successfully completed his mission from the twentieth century to Palestine at what appeared to be the appropriate time but to have quickly met a Jew, and a scribe at that. His luck took on added significance because he knew that Rome had divided Palestine into five provinces, Galilee, Samaria, Judea, Idumea and Perea, and of the two million people living in these provinces, only about half were Jews. The others were a mixture of Pagan Greeks, Romans, Syrians, Egyptians, Arabs, Persians, and Babylonians.

He was enjoying everything Ishmael had to say and he planned to encourage him to provide information in even greater detail. For the moment, though, certain questions burned inside him and he was trying to devise a means of asking them without making his young friend suspect that he was anything other than what he professed to be. He decided that by making himself as foreign as a foreigner could be he could ask Ishmael questions so basic that even most children would consider their answers to be common knowledge.

Ishmael was expounding on various priests' differences of opinion about the procedures that should be followed in disposing of a flawed scroll when Eric interrupted him.

"When we met this morning you asked me something that I didn't understand," Eric ventured. "Who is this expected one that you spoke of?"

"The Messiah, of course," Ishmael responded in a tone shaded with pity for Eric's ignorance. "The one that will be sent by God. The one who will free our people and be our king. A king mightier than even Solomon or David."

A wave of excitement exploded inside Eric. Only with great effort was he able to subdue it outwardly, as he received his first confirmation that he had, indeed, transported himself to Judea and, from Ishmael's remark, it was probably prior to, or during, the time of Jesus' ministry.

Trying to curb his enthusiasm, Eric continued his questioning. He knew the conversation could take a bad turn because, as a Pharisee who practiced strict adherence to the law, it was unlikely that Ishmael would have much tolerance for the interpretation his superiors had given to the teachings of Jesus.

"But how will you know him?" Eric asked. "Will he just appear out of the sky, or will it be in a blaze of glory behind the veil of the most holy in your temple?"

"No, no," Ishmael replied, with just a hint of superior tolerance. "Scripture tells us that he will be born of a woman and come out of Bethlehem, a descendent of the line of David. The law of Moses tells us that he cannot become a Rabbi until the age of thirty. Now everyone whose work it is to interpret the scriptures, and especially the chronology of Daniel, knows that he is here now and will reveal himself to us and the Romans at any time."

"Does your God have a name?" Eric asked.

"God revealed his name to Moses so that He would be distinguished from pagan gods, and so the nations would know that Israel's God was the one, true God. His name is so sacred that no one dare speak it except the High Priest on the Day of Atonement, when he prays, from the sanctuary of the holy of holies, for forgiveness for our nation's sins."

"But just where and how do you expect the Messiah to appear?" He asked, hoping that his pressure for details would not arouse Ishmael's anger or suspicion.

"We're not really sure," Ishmael continued, apparently not at all disturbed by Eric's curiosity. "It seems as of late that a new one crops up almost daily. They don't always claim outright to be the One; sometimes they just imply by innuendo and signs in order to build up a following, and then allow their followers to declare them to be the One. For this reason we are warned to be very skeptical and leery of those who profess to be the Messiah. One of them even walked into a synagogue and declared to the priest and everyone there that he was the One."

"Who was he, and how did the priests know that he wasn't the Messiah?" Eric asked, almost too quickly.

"Well, it happened a couple of years ago, and I've only heard the stories, but it seems that this man, who had been a carpenter, all of a sudden decides to walk into the synagogue in Nazareth on the Sabbath and started reading from the scroll of Isaiah where the Messiah is prophesied. After having read the passage he turned to the priests and declared that the prophecies he had just read had now been fulfilled in him. Well now, it appears that there was a great deal of shouting and name calling that followed this because, you see, it wasn't the first time they had encountered the blasphemous acts of this man; nor was it the last. He even declared himself equal to God and, the last I heard, to this day he wanders throughout Galilee performing magical tricks intended to give the appearance of curing the afflicted. He is assisted in this conspiracy by a group of followers who no doubt exchange ailments among themselves from city to city to ward off the boredom of being cured of the same impairment so often."

"Ishmael, you appear to be sincere in your disapproval of this person but how can you judge for certain? Have you had some personal experience with him?"

"I have not," Ishmael answered, somewhat irritated. "But I know that a priest speaks only the truth, and for this Jesus (it was the first time Ishmael had mentioned his name) to break God's laws under the pretext that HE takes the place of that law and so the law is no longer necessary, does not require a face-to-face confrontation with him to verify my disapproval."

"In what way did this Jesus, I think you called him, break the law?"

"If you are a stranger to our ways then how is it that you know about a veil covering the chamber of the most holy, which only the High Priest is allowed to enter?" Ishmael asked, catching Eric off guard.

"We have such a chamber in our houses of worship in my home land of Britannia, and I guess I just assumed that everyone else did too," he lied. Eric hated lying, and the unexpected question became an exercise in survival that taught him to be more careful of what he said.

"Britannica." Ishmael repeated the name. "I've heard of this place, but only tales of a barbarian tribe of people totally lacking in commercial or cultural progress. You do not appear to have come from such a place. Is it true what I have heard?"

"Many tales become distorted by those who repeat things they have not seen for themselves." If Ishmael caught the unspoken significance, he gave no indication.

Like most lies, Eric thought, his first would probably necessitate another, so he made an effort to steer the conversation away from the subject of Britannica."In my travels I have heard of this man you speak of. I have heard both good and bad and, if nothing else, he is certainly a subject for stimulating conversation. Which of the laws of Moses did you say he had broken?"

"Two of the greatest ten, as they were written in stone with God's own hand," Ishmael replied, with a somewhat dramatic deliverance as if rehearsing for some as yet unwritten sermon he would one day deliver.

"He actually advocated activity on the Sabbath in opposition to God's commandment, justifying it with his own logic that the Sabbath was made for man, and not man for the Sabbath. He even made tempting examples for those weaker souls who were eager to have an excuse to break laws. He tricked them into hypothetical situations, asking them if their prize animal fell into a stream on the Sabbath which of them would wait until the Sabbath passed to pull the animal out, lest he drown. These examples are traps designed by Satan to make men question God's wisdom."

"No offense intended, my friend Ishmael, I ask only to gain insight, but in your God's wisdom would it be in the best interest of either the shepherd or the sheep to allow the animal to drown?"

Ishmael was silent for a few seconds. Eric could see the color come into his face as he replied in a somewhat higher voice, "I do not question God's law. I only do my best to live by it."

"You mentioned there were two laws he broke," Eric continued, not wanting Ishmael's frustration to grow any greater on this subject of the Sabbath.

"Blasphemy.'

"Blasphemy?" He questioned.

"Yes, blasphemy," Ishmael repeated, "in that he has made himself equal to God."

"How did he accomplish this?"

"He didn't accomplish it, he only spoke it, stating that he and the Father are one."

"'That is indeed strange," Eric replied, "as it conflicts with the things I have heard that he has claimed pertaining to his relationship with your God. In all reports that I have been able to gather it has been said that he proclaims his father to be greater than he is. He says that he could do nothing on his own initiative, only that which his father had instructed him to do, and other expressions of that nature. I wonder, Ishmael, if it is possible that he meant that he and the Father were one in thought, as is the expression when two people are in total agreement?"

"How is it that you have so much information on this man when you are a stranger in this land?" Ishmael asked, with irritation noticeably growing in his voice.

"The internal unrest in Palestine is not an uncommon subject for conversation in other lands that I travel through, and this Jesus' name keeps popping up in the center of the turmoil," Eric said, perpetuating his lie.

"Perhaps the greatest proof I can offer that the man is a fool is that he not only offends Herod with this talk of being king, but he annoys the Romans as well, as it is said that Pilate himself is content with the present arrangement. But this man is not even satisfied to have just the armies of Rome and Herod Antipas as his adversaries. He has also declared his enmity with an even greater power. He has challenged the teachings of Caiaphas and the law itself, which is the same as challenging the word of God."

"As for myself, Ishmael, I would want to judge this man on the things I personally heard him say and on the works he does. In fact," Eric continued, "I'll probably make it a point while I am in Palestine to try to attend a gathering where this Jesus is teaching. Do you happen to know his location?" He asked, finally arriving at the question he had wanted to ask since he first laid eyes on Ishmael.

"I really have matters of much greater consequence to keep track of," replied Ishmael, "but the last report I heard of him placed him somewhere around Tiberias. But then, that was sometime ago," he hastened to add.

Ishmael had no more than finished his sentence when they rounded a sharp bend in the road past a hillside that had obscured the view ahead. At the bottom of the short but rather steep hill, where the road dipped into a dry wash, three people were struggling with little success to free an ox-drawn cart whose wheel had slipped off the eroded roadbed and wedged between two boulders. Ishmael and Eric quickened their pace in order to offer assistance to the distressed travelers. Eric was particularly jubilant at the prospect of meeting new people.

They exchanged greetings briefly and immediately set about the chore at hand; the problem was so obvious that no explanations were necessary.

Within a moment, however, Eric found himself wishing that he had thought before acting. Somewhere in his conversation with Ishmael and the excitement of seeing other people he had forgotten about his very first discovery yesterday - the featherweight boulders. An instant before any of the others put their shoulders to it. Eric gave the cart a lift in a forward motion that actually pushed the ox forward and sent the others sprawling. There was a moment of silence as the beast settled itself. An array of bodies lay scattered in the road in various positions.

The look of astonishment on their faces, and the way they slowly gazed at one another, told him he'd better come up with something fast. One by one their gazes fell upon Eric, the only one left standing, and the one exhibiting the fatuous expression of the proverbial boy having his infamous encounter with the cookie jar.

"Well," he said, and even the sound of his own voice sounded stupid to him, "I guess two more bodies really made a difference. Either that or your ox just reread his job description." They all continued to stare at him, and their looks served to assure him that his feelings of stupidity were not unfounded. I'm sure, he thought, that these people are about as familiar with a job description as they are with a transistor.

Eager to change the climate of the scene, he reached his hand out to the man on the ground staring up at him. "Here, let me help you up," he offered. Slowly the man reached for his hand. Eric was careful to grip gently and lift with equal care. He smiled and helped him brush some dust off before extending his hand to the second fallen victim. Once they were all on their feet he was about to resume his unsolicited dusting assistance when he accidentally brought down the hood that had half covered the face of one of the most extraordinarily beautiful women he had ever seen. With all that had happened to him in the past few hours the moment was even more ethereal. Mathematics and statistical probability were subjects he had spent a life time dealing with, and it flashed through his mind that if he spent his entire life standing on the corner of the busiest intersection of New York City he would probably not see a half dozen faces that possessed the totality of beauty of the face before him. Yet there he stood, transplanted somewhere in time to the middle of a wilderness, and the third human being he encounters is a woman whose face would surely have given Mark Antony cause to reconsider his feelings for Cleopatra.

The slightest hint of a smile crossed her lips at his clumsy attempt to pretend that he was really going to do something else with his hands other than touch her body.

"Thank you," she said in a voice and manner which instantly told him that there was no pretense about her.

How could he, in a few seconds, without the benefit of conversation, know that she was intelligent, sensitive, aware, yet unassuming? He wasn't sure how he knew about her. He just knew, and experience had taught him that's usually the surest way you have of knowing anything.

About that time Ishmael was recovering his dignity and the older man in charge of prodding the ox came scurrying around to the back of the cart to make sure everyone was alright. A brief inquiry reassured him, and in answer to his question about what had caused the wagon to suddenly lurch forward, Eric assured him that their previous efforts must have loosened the wheel enough so the extra effort to Ishmael and him made the cart move much more easily than they had expected. It may have been feeble but it seemed to have served best than no explanation at all.

When the older man asked if they would join them for the morning meal Eric quickly accepted, without waiting to learn the correct local protocol from Ishmael.

Two poles and a blanket formed an instant lean-to, which gave them shelter from a morning sun that promised a much greater display of its energies in the hours to come. After introductions all around they learned that the travelers were father, son, and daughter.

CHAPTER VI

As the lovely girl, whose name was Milcah, went about preparing the meal, her brother, Benjamin, and Ishmael reloaded the cart with the items that had been removed to lighten the load. Eric took the opportunity to chat with Havilah, a gentle, soft spoken man whose wife had died two years ago. He was taking his family back to his brother's house in Beersheba.

During the course of the meal he learned that Beersheba was about seven or eight western miles north of where they were. When he was alone he would be able to use his map to calculate the time and direction he had walked to make contact with the road and thus pretty well pinpoint the location of the boulder pile that concealed his capsule.

The food consisted of a hot meal mixture of some kind resembling mush, a large loaf of flat manna which they all shared, and warm water. It was bland, but very satisfying.

Havilah invited Eric and Ishmael to accompany them on the journey north. They needed to catch up to his brother with whom they had been traveling, but who had continued on with his party when their cart became stuck. Eric made no comment at the time, but couldn't help thinking that even allowing for unfamiliar customs he found it strange that anyone would leave his brother and family stuck in the desert without waiting to assist him.

When they resumed their journey after the meal Eric made it a point to walk beside Milcah.

"How far ahead do you estimate your uncle to be?" He asked, finally breaking the silence.

"They departed about one hour before you arrived." she replied.

"I am a visitor in your land, but may I ask if it is the custom of parties traveling together, especially family, to get left behind without assistance if trouble occurs?"

"It is the custom of my father's brother, Esau." There was a hint of disapproval in her voice.

"Would I be safe in assuming that your uncle is not one of your favorite relatives?"

"To speak harshly of my father's brother would be to bring disgrace upon my grandparents."

"Even so, Milcah, history teaches us that from the time of Cain there have been members of the same family who have not always displayed equal integrity."

"Abandonment of one's family while traveling weighs but lightly on the conscience of one so lacking in integrity that they would steal their own brother's inheritance."

"Your uncle did that?"

"My father would admonish me if he knew that I spoke of this matter to a stranger. Please let us speak of it no more."

"I seek not to delve into your family's personal matter, but only to learn how in this land it is possible for this to happen. Won't you please tell me the circumstances that made this possible?"

Hesitantly she began, "My father, who is the oldest son, had until four years ago always attended his father's sheep and cattle, as well as his fields. Then my grandfather asked him to take his family and journey south into Egypt where he had heard of new vineyards and orchards, so that he might reside there and learn of these things and in time bring the knowledge and young saplings and vines back to Beersheba. Two weeks ago, my uncle, along with several of my grandfather's man slaves, visited us in Egypt. He informed us of my grandfather's death and bore proof of this sole inheritance of the estate. He explained that my grandfather believed that my father and his family had died of the same affliction that carried off my mother. He went on to explain that a message from an Egyptian neighbor informed them of this, but he had promised their mother that he would journey to Egypt to verify the tragedy, and thus he found us, alive. Now, my father is obligated to obey him as his master and we are returning to my uncle's home."

"But surely this will be corrected when it is known that your father and his family are alive!"

"A death bed blessing, once given, is irrevocable even by the one administering it. Besides, my father is a very good and kind man. It will be enough for him to have my grandmother know that he and her grandchildren are not dead."

"But what if..."

"Please," she interrupted, "I feel ashamed. I have used you as a vessel in which to pour out my own poison, which has been locked up inside me. I ask your forgiveness and I ask further that we speak no more of this matter."

They walked the next mile or so in silence. The only sound was the squeaking of the heavy cart wheels crying out for a fresh application of animal fat, and an occasional fly, whose singular goal in life seemed to revolve around some sort of fetish with the human ear.

It was Benjamin who broke the silence as he pointed ahead and shouted back to them, "Esau, Esau." He had reached the crest of a small hill that allowed visibility for several miles. When the others arrived they could see a party of six people and three wagons about a half mile ahead. This time, it appeared, it was they who were broken down.

Fifteen or twenty minutes later they arrived at a scene of great confusion, straining and grunting. A small man with a large nose and even larger voice, who could only have been Esau, was shouting orders at several men who were trying to guide a newly repaired wheel onto the axle, while the others held up the crippled side of the emptied wagon.

Havilah greeted his brother and started to introduce Ishmael and Eric, but Esau quickly pointed out the foolishness of his priorities and ordered him and Benjamin to assist the men with the repairs.

Eric was positive that even if he hadn't heard Milcah's story Esau would have made a bad first impression on him.

Ishmael and Eric pitched in and within seconds the wheel was in place. Only then, by way of curt gestures, did Esau give Havilah permission to resume his introductions.

"Tell me, merchant," Esau asked, "what kind of goods do you deal in?"

"Only those of a limited and exclusive nature to be beheld by royalty and heads of state," Eric stated with deliberate pomposity.

"Really," replied Esau, "spoken with the true tongue of a merchant. A statement designed to whet the appetite of the fools you seek out as prospective clients!"

Ishmael surprised Eric when he spoke up. "He speaks the truth. Last night I saw by accident what surely could have only been meant for the eyes of the high priest; only he could explain its wonders!"

Eric shuddered at Ishmaels well intended rebuttal, and could only hope that he wouldn't elaborate further on the things he had seen. Fortunately, Esau was more interested in scoring points with his sarcasm than he was in the specifics of Eric's products.

"Is this apprentice a part of your act?" Esau snickered. "If you deal in objects of such value, how is it you do not travel under the protection of a caravan?"

"The products and services that I deal in would be of no value to anyone without the knowledge of how to put them to use," Eric said. "Besides, it should be of little concern to you, since nothing will be presented to you for your consideration of purchase."

"Another vendors trick designed to whet the appetite." Esau snorted, but Eric could tell that he had pushed a button.

"No," he replied," just a matter of economics." With that, Eric turned and walked back toward Havilah's cart where he saw Milcah smiling that same smile that came only from her eyes and not her lips.

Esau's slaves were just finishing reloading the plants, the fruits of Havilah's labor, back onto the wagon as Esau shouted at them to hurry up and get underway.

They traveled for about an hour more before making a camp of lean-tos to shelter them from the worst of the midday sun. This time Milcah took it upon herself to sit next to Eric beside their cart.

"It appears that you and my uncle did not strike up an immediate friendship."

"Forgive me, Milcah, the word will mean nothing to you, but the only appropriate word I can think of to describe your uncle is a bunghole." He spoke the word in English. Eric was not one who depended upon profanity to express himself but in this case Esau seemed so deserving of the title that any less derogatory expression would be inappropriate.

"You are correct," Milcah said, "it is a word I have not heard before. What does it mean?"

"Yes, merchant, please enlighten us both as to the meaning of this word," Esau said as he rounded the corner of their lean-to.

"I was unaware that you were listening to our conversation," Eric said. "It's just as well, because I never would have chosen to address you with this title as I could see that you are a man who is skeptical of flattery, and I suspect you are already familiar with its meaning."

"I seem to recall hearing it, but refresh my memory as to its origin and meaning."

"It is a word from Britannica paying honor to a man who is most noble but not of royal blood. No higher title can be given," Eric explained, with an agonizingly straight face.

"Yes, of course. Now I remember," Esau lied.

"Your niece has told me of your recent elevation in stature and I was suggesting to her that it might be appropriate for her and the others to address you with this title to show their respect."

"I don't believe that will be necessary," Esau said, although he was obviously delighted with the idea. "Perhaps, though, there would be times when it would be appropriate." He paused in thought. "Perhaps in the presence of others. Let me think on it. We will talk later, merchant," Esau said as he turned and left for the shade of his own lean-to.

Eric could feel Milcah's stare on him as he watched Esau walk away. He turned to meet her eyes.

"Who are you really?" She asked, catching him unprepared for the question.

"Only a traveling merchant in a strange land."

"Ishmael thinks you are something more. He says you are capable of doing wondrous things."

"Ishmael witnessed me using some highly sophisticated toys designed to amuse the rich." They must be very heavy toys indeed."

"What do you mean?" Eric replied, with a quizzical glance.

"Only a few minutes ago I tried to move your pack under the wagon, out of the sun, and it was as if it were affixed to the earth. I could not budge it."

"I'm afraid, Milcah, that if you fell victim to a rather sophisticated theft deterrent device that renders the pack practically immovable." Eric again suffered the discomfort brought on by a lie.

"And our cart that was hopelessly stuck until you nearly sent our ox flying with your push?"

"We all contributed to that," he said, rather unconvincingly. She just stared at him with a look that told him in no uncertain terms that she wasn't buying a thing he was saying.

"All right," he said, "there are some things that I just can't go into right now, but I promise you, we will talk more about them later. Earlier today I honored your request to speak no more of a subject. Could you see your way to return the favor?"

"Of course," she said, "but I will hold you to your promise."

"You can count on it," he smiled.

'There is one thing I would like to know, however, which I do not believe you have any reason to withhold from me."

"What's that?"

"In spite of what you convinced my uncle of, I would like to know the true meaning of the word 'bunghole'." (She pronounced it perfectly.)

"Oh little Milcah, please, I'm afraid I allowed myself to be upset by your uncle. What I said was in poor taste and I would hope that you would allow the meaning of the word to remain a mystery, since it has no meaning in your tongue."

"I would think that my concession to drop one subject would entitle me at least to an honest meaning of a foreign word."

"All right, you win. But let me think of how to put this into words." He took a few seconds to collect his thoughts, and then began hesitantly. "I think the best way to describe it would be to have you imagine that part of one's body that is the last thing to have contact with yesterday's digested dinner."

She stared at him with a blank expression for a few seconds, then her eyes widened; she gulped, and placed her hand over her mouth to partially hide her shocked face!

Oh lord, what have I done, he thought. As Eric looked at her face he watched the look of horror transform itself into an outburst of giggling and then uncontrolled laughter.

Milcah's laughter was so contagious that Eric couldn't help but join her, and the two of them sat there in the vastness of the Judean wilderness shaking with laughter and wiping tears from their eyes.

"Oh, please don't let him decide that he wants us to address him in such a manner, for I would surely be betrayed by my own giddiness," Milcah said, dabbing at her eyes with her scarf.

"Your uncle will undoubtedly feel that his niece possesses a consistently cheerful disposition, especially when addressing him."

"More than likely he will feel that the desert sun has taken its toll on my brain."

They laughed until their sides could tolerate no more.

The worst of the high noon sun had passed, and the sound of the lean-tos being broken down and stowed in the carts indicated that it was time for them to do the same and resume the journey. Although the hysteria of their laughing jag had died down, neither of them had gotten the benefit of a nap, as did the others. Each time they tried, Milcah would form a new image of where the use of her new-found foreign word might be applied in connection with her uncle. This inevitability resulted in a muffled snicker which was echoed by Eric as he tried to imagine what scene of nonsense she had conjured up this time. For the next few minutes they each would engage in a desperate attempt to suppress and mute their giggling. With each new eruption Milcah whispered how shameless and immoral she felt her behavior to be.

For his part, Eric chose to put aside all his thoughts of greater magnitude for some other time and simply enjoy this moment of nonsense.

Now that they were up and moving they walked in silence, in contrast to their giddy rest period. Eric contemplated the act of deception performed by one brother against the other, all in the interest of improving one's lot in life with no apparent thought given to either God or man's concept of right and wrong. Why did he find it so strange that an occurrence of this nature was not reserved for corrupt twentieth century business tycoons and politicians? After all, incidents of far more ingenious conniving than this had been recorded centuries ago. Although the motives differed greatly, he recalled the Biblical account of Rebekah's manipulation of Isaac's blessing to fall upon Jacob instead of Esau, as Isaac had intended. Even though it suited God's purpose, was that not deception?

The coincidence was beginning to build. If his recollection was correct, the incident took place very near where they were since Isaac, the son of Abraham, had resided in Beersheba.

Was it only chance that Havilah's brother's name was Esau? Then an idea began to take shape.

How often in life have we seen injustices occur that we would like to be able to correct but lack the means to do so? Well, here he was in an era where the simple use of a match would leave those witnessing it spellbound and his pack contained enough scientific hardware to impress even a twentieth century layman. How immoral would it be, he thought, if he were to use some of those gadgets to right a wrong in the interest of justice? Besides, what could happen to him if he got caught? Possibly anything from a position in

Herod's court to public stoning as a demonic heretic! He quickly disregarded the last possibility and began to formulate a plan.

During the next travel break Eric hurriedly slipped far enough away from the rest to be out of hearing range. There he quickly began rigging remote control devices and recording into his recorder. The party had already begun to move on before he finished, and as he came over the rise he could see Milcah and Ishmael looking over their shoulders for him. He ran to catch up, but offered no excuse for his delay when he rejoined them, even though he wanted to. They were both too tactful to mention it, he realized in another flashing thought of silliness, but why else would they imagine him to be delayed so long except for some marathon session of bodily functions.

This childish thought passed along with the day as sunset found them still about four miles from Beersheba. They pulled the wagons up a draw that led to a shallow dead end canyon about a quarter mile off the road. There was little for Eric to do as the servants prepared the camp. Servants, let alone slaves, was a side of life that Eric had never been exposed to. They made him feel "unnecessary."

The barren Judean wilderness offered little in the way of hospitality to trespassers. There was no wood or even twigs to gather. They started a fire with twigs and what he guessed to be dried camel chips that they had been transporting for the entire journey.

It felt great just to slip out of his heavy backpack, kick back and watch the activity going on around him. The realization of what had happened to him still seemed like part of a dream. He rubbed his chin, examined his hands, breathed in the smell of the fire, and reassured himself that these senses do not function so vividly in a dream. There was even one morbid instant when the thought flashed through his mind that all of these people he was watching as they carried out the chores pertinent to this day of their lives, in this time and place, were in reality already dead and long forgotten in some unmarked grave. Why, he wondered, did

70

that thought seem so unreal. It just didn't fit. Surely relativity relates to reality! Reality dictates that this is here and now. Life in the twentieth century is what was unreal.

There goes your warped little sicko brain again, Corbett, he told himself. Why don't you stick to questions that you might possibly understand instead of always going over to play in "never- never land."

And another thing: In the interests of science why don't you pay more attention to the culture and customs of camp life on a Judean caravan instead of just watching every move that gorgeous creature makes? At last he had finally dealt himself a question that he knew EXACTLY how to answer.

After the evening meal Eric made a point of positioning his bedroll far enough from the others so he would not be detected in the middle of the night when he intended to put his plan into action. In the darkness there was no risk in slipping on his wristwatch that would silently awaken him in four hours by applying a gentle prickling action to his wrist.

Laying there under his bedroll, the desert air took on a welcome coolness that he could not have imagined earlier in the heat of the day. His eyes fixed on the night sky, he had never seen so many stars shining with such distinct clarity, unobscured by the contamination of modern civilization. Even with all he had to reflect upon, he found his mind giving way to welcome waves of drowsiness as he drifted into a dream-filled sleep.

He soon found himself in the back seat of his father's 1949 Buick, distinguishable only by its rear window and its door handle to which, somehow, the belt loop of his pants and become hopelessly entangled. Sally Eckhart, the girl to whom he had surrendered his virginity, was impossibly enmeshed beneath him in those close quarters as he struggled feverishly to get his pants on before the approaching figure of Reverend Schroder could reach the window.

In the asymmetrical fragmentation of dreams that offers no explanation as to their reason or pattern, and without knowing the outcome of his prior dilemma, he found himself in a different setting. This time he was behind the wheel of

71

his new Oldsmobile, zipping along in freeway traffic and introducing Milcah, his awestruck passenger, to the wonders of twentieth century civilization. Her eyes were like saucers as she drank in the towering buildings and the oncoming traffic. Her small fingers clutched the seat and dashboard as she tried to comprehend how it was possible to move at such blinding speeds.

He was trying to convince Milcah that there wasn't a man concealed behind the dashboard who was responsible for the voice she heard speaking in the strange language. As he reached to flip the car radio to a music station he was brought back to the reality of the Judean desert by the nudging of his alarm clock.

As he opened his eyes there was an instant when he had to determine which WAS reality - that freeway or this desert. The instant passed.

He shut off the alarm and surveyed the camp to make sure the others were sound asleep. He felt a slight adrenalin surge, the way one does in those seconds of waiting just prior to embarking upon some feat that involves a certain element of risk. He quickly gathered what he needed out of his pack and headed down to a point out of view of the camp near where the wagons had left the road.

He dug a shallow hole and laid the recorder in it. He placed four small stones around the hole, than positioned a large, flat rock on top of them to allow the sound to escape clearly. In front of this he dug another hole in which he placed an igniter and a combination of flash powder and combustible fluids (all part of the testing chemicals he had brought with him). When he finished, he headed back to camp.

He found a spot near a rock about twenty-five feet from where Esau lay sleeping. A small piece of infrared lens allowed him to watch the effect as he whispered Esau's name over and over again into a miniaturized directional beam voice gun.

Esau finally stirred and looked around him as one would when half wakened by a dream. Eric continued talking soothingly so that the poor man would not run off screaming into the desert. He instructed him to rise and walk to the point where they had left the road to make camp.

Esau was visibly shaken but only whispered one question, "Who are you?"

"Esau," Eric replied, "you are awake. You are not dreaming. You will ask no further questions. You will do only exactly what I instruct you to do."

At this, Esau gave a wide eyed nod of agreement as he slowly got up and headed toward the spot near the road where Eric had directed him.

The night was fairly dark so it was easy for Eric to follow at a safe distance. When Esau drew near the spot where the recorder had been placed Eric found himself desperately wishing that he had had an opportunity to test the "special effects" he had so hastily rigged. No time for rehearsals, he thought, as he pushed the first of two buttons on his remote control unit.

The immediate area lit up in a flash of light as a large ball of smoke rose into the desert night air leaving beneath it a pit of dancing blue flames.

Esau jumped back and fell to the ground. Too frightened to let out a yell or even move, he just sat there staring at the fire. Perfect, Eric thought, as he pushed the other button.

The recorder started and Eric heard his own voice doing his impression of an off-screen voice in an old Cecil B. DeMille movie.

"Esau," the voice boomed forth, "for the sake of your niece Milcah, who has found favor in my eyes, I have decided to bestow mercy upon you and extend to you a final opportunity to redeem your very soul. It is indeed an act of undeserved kindness, as you have earned my wrath by the unscrupulous acts of treachery you have perpetrated against your brother Havilah to rob him of his birthright."

Esau sat staring in a terrorized trance as the voice continued.

"At dawn's first light you will go to your brother and, in front of witnesses, give back to him by declaration that which is rightfully his. You will ask your brother for forgiveness and, if he bestows it upon you then I, too, will bestow my forgiveness upon you. Go now into the desert and pray and speak not one word until you see the rays of the morning sun. Then you will do as I have instructed you. Go, and do not look back upon this place lest you suffer the same fate that fell upon the wife of my servant, Lot. Go," came the final command.

With this, Esau got to his feet and started walking slowly out into the desert without looking back.

As soon as he was sure that Esau had gone off a safe distance Eric retrieved his recorder, moved the boulder, and filled in the holes, leaving no trace of what had occurred there. He then returned to camp, put his watch and other items back into his pack, and climbed into his bedroll.

He couldn't fall right back to sleep. Something was nagging at him. Sure, he reasoned, Esau was a thief who deserved to be the victim of that somewhat terrifying deception, but was he the one to make that judgment? Would God approve of his methods? On the other hand, he consoled himself, the recording never came right out and said that it was God.

Wrestling with these questions and searching for self-approval kept Eric from falling asleep for the hour or so that was left of the night.

As the still Judean desert began to grow lighter Eric could make out in the distance the lone figure of Esau as he made his way back towards camp.

Convinced by now that he had done the right thing, Eric waited to see the results of his theatrics.

The camp was still sleeping soundly when Esau arrived, but he soon had everyone awake and on their feet. He gathered them all together, including his manservants, and told them he had something very important to announce.

As they all waited, Eric saw Milcah give him a curious glance, which as much as asked if he knew what this was all about.

"Last night," Esau began, "Jehovah saw fit to reveal Himself to me."

Everyone in the group began looking at one another.

"I do not know why He favored me," he continued, "but I do know that I cannot serve Him and also bear the burden of running a household. I therefore declare, with all of you as my witnesses, that I am transferring full and complete ownership of our father's estate to my brother Havilah. I ask only that he bestow upon me publicly his best wishes and his forgiveness."

There was only silence. The whole camp was shocked by what they had just heard.

"What say you, my brother?" Esau asked.

"I don't know what to say," Havilah said, confused. "Are you sure you know what you're saying? Perhaps you had nothing more than a very real dream."

"It was no dream," Esau assured him. "He awakened me and sent me to another place down near the road where he spoke to me out of a fire that burned with a blue flame...Havilah," Esau's voice grew higher, "because I have done all this for you, it is important that you say in public that you forgive me!"

"Esau, my brother," Havilah said quietly, "I had already forgiven you before you did this, but, if it is important to you that I make a public declaration then I will say, in front of all those present, that I forgive you."

"Oh thank you, my brother!" cried Esau. "Does that mean that I can still reside in our father's house, which is now yours?"

"You will be welcome there all the days of your life, my brother."

"Then it is done," Esau said. "When we arrive in Beer-sheba I will inform the authorities."

The two brothers embraced, which was a signal to the rest that they were free to go about their business.

The servants seemed confused by this sudden change of authority, not knowing who they should serve first with the morning meal and chores, so they finally just did what was needed to get the caravan organized, with a minimum of fuss and formality.

Ishmael asked Eric if he believed such an incident had really taken place, and Eric answered with some time-honored tripe like, "Who are we to say?"

Milcah came up and stared deep into Eric's eyes. Finally she said, "I don't have the slightest idea how, but, I am positive that in some way you had something to do with this." Eric offered no reply, and she turned and went over to embrace her father.

They broke camp and later that morning found themselves within view of Beersheba, even then, one of the oldest and most historic cities in the world.

CHAPTER VII

Eric eagerly accepted an invitation to spend the night as a guest in Havilah's newly acquired house. Ishmael declined, as he was anxious to return to his duties and could probably cover half the distance between Beersheba and Edh Dhahriye before dark.

Eric could feel his excitement growing with every step they took nearer the city gates. He was actually going to see for himself a civilization that other scientists could only speculate on as they cleaned and cataloged some long-buried shard of pottery.

Just outside the city there was a large area of stalls, corrals, booths and sheds. People there were conducting business, and occasionally a pair of Roman soldiers could be seen milling through the crowd. Eric thought that perhaps he was seeing one of the earliest examples of "suburban sprawl," a shopping center located outside the center of town. As it turned out, though, it was a holding area for animals and goods upon which the owners had not yet paid the tax that would allow them to trade within the city.

"Just another ingenious method the Romans have devised to further wring the country dry," Ishmael explained. "The new tax came as a surprise to many farmers, shepherds and merchants who were coming to town for the first time since it was enacted, and they were unable to pay until after they had sold what they had brought to the city. Fortunately, by the grace of Caesar, Rome provided this area where they might, for a fee, store their goods until they found a customer." Eric could feel the anger and frustration growing in Ishmael's voice as he spoke.

"It's like a huge pawn shop," Eric said.

"A what?" asked Ishmael.

"Just an expression they use in Ethiopia," Eric shrugged, attempting to make it not worthwhile for Ishmael to pursue any further explanation. He reminded himself again to try to avoid words when he was unsure of their Aramaic interpretation.

"The merchants in the city are unhappy," Ishmael continued, "because many of their prospective customers come out here seeking bargains. Those caught out here in the Roman trap are unhappy because by the time they have paid the tax and storage fees they are left with nearly nothing. The only ones to show a clear gain, of course, are our Roman benefactors."

Although a man of God, Ishmael carried so much rage inside him that Eric could easily picture him dressed in a T-shirt and Levis on the Berkeley campus in the 1960's, or in the I.R.A., P.L.O., J.D.F., as a young warrior with Geronimo, a Minute Man at Bunker Hill, or in any one of the thousands of causes, large or small, right or wrong, that angry young men have been involved in since who knows when. It seemed to Eric that nothing had changed except the names and the weapons. (What was that old song that went, "The answer, my friend, is blowin' in the wind"...)

"There is little one can do against the power of Rome," Eric said.

"But Caesar's power will crumble before the might of the Messiah when he arrives," he paused, "and he will arrive soon. Then the Roman soldiers will scurry out of Judea like hordes of wounded pigs, trampling one another under their own horses' hooves in order to flee his wrath."

"Ishmael," Eric hesitated, then began again, "I hope you will allow me to visit you in Edh Dhahriye when I continue my journey. I would like to speak to you at greater length about the expectations you have of the Messiah and what God's purpose for him might be."

"I will look forward to your visit with great anticipation, Eric. Especially in view of the fact that you have promised a further demonstration of some of the wondrous trade items you deal in."

A thought suddenly occurred to Eric that sent him running to see Esau, breaking off in the middle of Ishmael's sentence.

"Esau," he asked, trying to seem a great deal less concerned than he really was, "what can one expect at the gate? Do the soldiers go through even a man's personal effects?" The thought of a Roman soldier going through his pack like a customs inspector was a prospect he was not at all prepared to deal with.

"No," replied Esau. "Besides, I know the one on the left. His name is Jepher, and he has fallen asleep more than one night with the taste of my wine on his lips. He will pass us through with no more than a token glance into the carts."

In spite of what Eric thought of Esau he suddenly found himself feeling quite grateful to him for whatever minor corruption or back scratching he might have previously engaged in with the Roman soldiers. That's another thing that hasn't changed much, Eric thought, "juice" still makes the difference.

It was as Esau said. They passed through the gate without incident. Once inside the city, Eric's eyes darted everywhere. He gawked like a person seeing for the first time in his life.

The first impression he registered was how small everything was. The doorways seemed small, the ceilings low, and the streets narrow. Dirty, but healthy looking children scurried everywhere, stopping just long enough to stare at the strangers passing by. After they left the main street with its street vendors they went through some passageways that were barely wide enough to allow the carts to pass.

Then the street widened out into an area bounded by walls on both sides with doors spaced at various intervals. The greater the distance between the doors meant the larger the house behind that section of wall and, thus, the richer the person dwelling there.

Eric used his "stranger from another land" routine to good advantage as he questioned Ishmael and Milcah about even the most trivial things along the way.

The door to Havilah's house opened onto a courtyard. Entering, they were met by a middle-aged woman who was soon joined by two younger women. Their initial greetings were to Esau and he quietly took the occasion to explain the situation to them and introduce his brother as their new master.

After they shared some refreshments they said their farewells to Ishmael, and Eric reconfirmed his commitment to visit him on his way north to Jerusalem.

When Ishmael had left one of the young women showed Eric to his room, stating that she would return soon with his water.

The room, overlooking the courtyard from the second story, was small but immaculate, and there was a shuttered door that opened onto a small balcony. There was no closet, and the total contents of the room consisted of a reed woven mat, one blanket, a small wooden stool, and a table that held a water bowl and a bronze oil lamp. He didn't think AAA would rank it next to the Hilton but, from what he had seen coming through town, this would be considered a very well-to-do household. Besides, the sheer delight of taking off his backpack was sure to be among the highlights of this or any other day.

Eric was standing on the small balcony overlooking a narrow alley that was void of any activity when the girl returned with a pitcher of water and a towel. She placed them on the table and left the room without a word.

He was sure that the pitcher of water was not intended for anything more than freshening up, but since he had no idea when his next opportunity would be to take a bath he stripped down and had more fun than a sparrow in a birdbath.

Damn, he thought, why did I scratch a deodorant stick off the "absolutely necessary" list when planning the contents of the backpack? He felt very refreshed as he climbed into the one change of robes he had brought with him.

There was no way he was going to be able to sleep before dinner, as he was being swept along in a current of exuberance that he felt only a handful of people who had ever lived could relate to. Some members of that exclusive club might be Glenn, Armstrong, Einstein, Curie, Hillary, Galileo, or, for that matter, probably any woman who has ever given birth. So much for exclusiveness, he smiled to himself. Anyway, now would be a good opportunity to record some of his notes.

He dug his recorder out of his pack, made himself as comfortable as the small wooden cot would allow, and began transferring his experiences onto tape, beginning with his startling encounter with Ishmael.

He was less than five minutes into his dictation when he was interrupted by a gentle tapping at the door. He quickly shoved the recorder under the blanket and, opening the door, was surprised to see Milcah standing there. They stood awkwardly staring at each other for several seconds before Milcah asked, "May I come in?"

"Please do," Eric said, opening the door wider. "Won't you sit down?" He said, gesturing rather nervously toward the small stool.

"Thank you," Milcah replied in a much more comfortable manner than his.

"Well now, what can I do for you?" Recognizing the lack of profundity in his opening remark he tried to analyze why he was feeling ill at ease with Milcah there in his room.

"Well, for one thing, you can relax a little. The whole household is asleep and surely by now you must be used to my unmaidenly forwardness. You did, however, promise me some answers, so I have come to collect. You do pay that which you have promised, do you not, Eric?"

"What is it you want to know?" - his uneasiness diminishing.

"I want to know who you really are."

"I'm just a man, like so many other men, in search of understanding," he answered, with all the conviction of a school boy lying to his teacher.

"I know of no other man," Milcah began, with a hint of irritation in her voice, "who carries a pack that weighs as much as a camel, who dislodges a cart that an ox has failed to budge, and who I also believe to have been instrumental, in some way, with my uncle's nocturnal encounter with God. Your promise to me," she continued in a somewhat softer manner, "was for truth. If you are going to tell me that you are like other men, then there is no need to ask you additional questions, for surely the rest of them would also be followed by lies. Eric," she paused for a few seconds before continuing, "I release you from your promise. I do not want you to tell me anything that your heart tells you not to. But I, too, am searching for something, and with so many things in conflict with each other it often makes the truth appear so illusive that mere mortals surly are not capable of understanding it. That is why, when I came to your door just now and heard the same thing Ishmael said he had heard - that you speak in tongues, I thought perhaps you could be the one to help me in my search."

It was obvious to Eric that this was not "reverse psychol-ogy" or any other subterfuge. Milcah was dealing in pure honesty.

"Your intuitions are correct, Milcah. There are some things about me that are different than other men. But it could cause me a great deal of difficulty if this should be found out. Because of my promise I will tell you as much as I feel you can comprehend but, believe me, your greatest scholars and wisest men would find their minds boggled by the things I will be telling you."

"I would never do anything to cause you any difficulty, Eric. I hope you believe that."

"I, too, have intuitions and I know that you would not deceive me. But I have to warn you that the things I am about to tell you may cause you to doubt my sanity."

"Please, Eric, it is important to me, and I promised not to judge you insane."

"Let me begin," Eric started, "by telling you that it was not exactly a lie when I told you that I was a man in search of understanding, for that is really the purpose of my being here. But something you said a few moments ago about your own search for truth causes me to believe that in some strange way, no matter how different our methods or circumstances may be, our objectives might be the same. Please tell me, Milcah, what it is you keep looking for that remains clouded by conflict?"

Milcah was starting straight ahead as if in a trance as she began to speak. "It has to do with a man that I have heard about but have never seen. A shepherd boy named Yiar told me about him over a year ago and he spoke of the wonderful things that he said and did. The look in his eyes when he spoke of him told me that this man, also, was no ordinary man. At the time, Yiar and his family were far to the north near Tiberias, but his brother, Maayan, spoke of hearing priests and others condemn this same man for being a false prophet and a heretic. Since then he has been much talked about, but those who would seem to have good things to say about him appear to be afraid to speak out in the face of popular opinion. It is said that he has spoken out against the high priests, Herod, and even Pilate, who is himself Rome. Of the two brothers bearing witness to him there was a great difference of opinion and, as I believe with all my heart that the teachings of Moses are true, and that because of His covenant with Abraham we are indeed God's chosen people..." she broke her trance and looked into Eric's eyes, "how is it, then, that I can feel this love and compassion toward this man who I have never seen and who the priests say is in opposition to Jehovah?" Her magnificent brown eyes locked with his for a long moment and then she finished, quietly stating, "That then is the conflict of my search for truth."

"His name," Eric said, cupping her face in his hands, "what is his name?"

"His name is Jesus," she said, her eyes beginning to well up with tears, "or at least it was. I'm not even sure he is still alive. That is one reason I was so happy to come to a large city like Beersheba where I can hear all of the latest news about what is happening throughout the land."

"He IS still alive," Eric said, dropping his hands. "And maybe, with just a little bit of luck, someday soon you and I will both see him."

"How do you know he is still alive? Have you heard recent news of his whereabouts?" Milcah asked anxiously.

Eric had already decided by the invocation of trust derived from some totally inexplicable source that if there were to be any risks involved in revealing his secret to Milcah betrayal would not be one of them. He would hold nothing back from her.

"No," Eric replied, "my news is about 2000 years old. But then, that's all part of the many things we are going to talk about if you still think you can handle it."

"You already have left me bewildered with your riddles of 2000 years and something about a handle."

"Let me try again," Eric said. "I'll try to make things as clear as I possibly can. I have constructed a machine," he began methodically, "capable of traveling through time. Backward is a matter of record now; forward is still untested. I was born nearly 2000 years from now and have managed to travel backwards in time to arrive in this designated place in the earth's history so that I might observe for myself how things were, or are, as the case might be, at that, or this, time."

The look on Milcah's face told Eric that in spite of his best efforts he was still trying to over-explain. "KISS" he repeated under his breath, "Keep-It-Simple-Stupid."

"I am from 2000 years into the future, Milcah, and, as far as I know, I am the first person to have unlocked the secret of traveling into a different time dimension."

"Eric," Milcah interrupted slowly, "your eyes tell me that you are speaking what you believe to be the truth, but what you are saying to me is that you have traveled here in something called a machine, from a time that has not yet happened? Is that what you just told me, Eric?"

"I also warned you that it would be difficult to comprehend."

"Difficult!" Milcah would have been yelling except for the necessity of not waking the household. "Eric, how is it possible to make yesterday happen again if it has already happened?"

"The technology is such that even in an era of high technology only a few minds could understand the process, so to explain it to you would only tend to confuse you more."

"Very well, Eric. Let me see if I can understand it better if I ask you some specific questions."

"Go right ahead," Eric nodded. "That might be a better way of doing it."

"First of all, what is a machine?"

The question was so elementary that it took a few seconds for Eric to realize just how intelligent it really was.

"A machine," he began, after some thought, "is a structure or vessel of some kind that usually consists of many moving parts. It is designed and built to do some kind of work. Your father's cart, in a way, is a machine. It has moving parts and is designed to transport people or goods from place to place."

"I do not think that my father's cart could take me to see Moses, but then I will assume that your machine has many more moving parts, that allow it to do many different things." Somehow Milcah managed to say that without the slightest bit of sarcasm in her voice. "Where is this machine now, and why do you journey on foot?"

"There are indeed many different machines that do different things. The one I came to Judea in is sitting in the desert about twenty kilometers from the place where Ishmael and I came across your party."

"Someday I would truly like to see this wondrous machine with all its moving parts, but enough talk of machines, let us speak now of where this machine brought you from. Are you from the lands north of Rome near the edges of the earth where it is said that people have yellow hair? Or from the East, where they tell tales of people whose eyes tilt upward and dress in clothing made from a worm?"

"Milcah," Eric said with a sigh, "you beautiful, intelligent creature, this is where things are really going to get tough."

He took her hand and led her to the cot where they both sat down. "Let me start by saying," Eric began, not at all sure where he was going, "that there are no edges on the earth. The earth is round, like a ball, and way on the other side of this giant ball, across a very large ocean, is another large land that will not even be discovered by people of this land for another 1500 years. It will be called America. That is where I come from."

"Eric," Milcah voiced an apologetic interruption, "I'm trying very hard to understand, but surely you would have to know that if the earth were a ball, those near the edges would slide down, and if this America you come from is on the other side it must be the bottom side, and what would keep a person there from falling off while walking upside down?"

"The earth has a force," Eric continued, "that is called "gravity." If you hold a pebble in your hand and turn your hand over, gravity is what makes it fall to the ground instead of going up. Even if you throw the pebble up, gravity brings it down again. Gravity also keeps people stuck to the surface of the earth. No matter what part of the ball you're on, the sky is always up and the earth is always down, so standing in America is just like standing here."

Bewilderment was written all over Milcah's face as she spoke. "I would truly like to see for myself some of the things of which you speak. A land where you stand upside down and feel no effects of it. Machines that move you without oxen or horses. It requires a great deal of faith to believe these things without seeing them."

"Faith is something I know very little about," Eric sighed. "In fact you could say that it is because of my inability to accept things on faith, without proof, that I traveled here. You see, Milcah, this man Jesus that you spoke of will be written about by his followers, and these writings will survive for centuries in the future. His teachings will be known by most of the world, and great churches will be established in his name. I felt that if somehow I could just talk to him, if only for a few moments, I would be able to know if all the things written about him are true and, thus, if all the things he said were going to happen really will happen. That is why, tomorrow, I start my journey north in search of him."

In a period of time that lasted no longer than a heartbeat Milcah made a decision that was totally foreign to the clear, solid, well thought out process she normally invoked prior to acting. By some inner compulsion that she could not have begun to explain, even to herself, she knew instantly what she must do. Had the compulsion not been so overwhelming she surely would have reasoned that she was having a conversation with a madman and done the sensible thing: smile calmly and make a discrete retreat out of the room. But the instant held no room for reason. There was only the one insistent fact that would give way to no other. Somehow, someway, she must make the journey with him. "Oh Eric, please, take me with you!" Her voice was filled with excitement.

"That's impossible. The journey will be long and probably dangerous. If anyone should even suspect that I am 'different' than they are, things could get a little hectic."

"But Eric, don't you see, I could help minimize the chance of that happening. You are a stranger in the land. You know little of our customs. People look at you because you are tall, your hair and skin are lighter than other men's, and you pronounce many words strangely. How could you expect to journey through this land asking questions and remain unnoticed?"

"I'm sorry, Milcah, it's just out of the question, and I'm sure your father would be the first to agree with me... his unmarried daughter traveling with a man unchaperoned."

"My father would never deny me anything that I felt so strongly about. And I would have thought, with your quest, that you would understand better than anyone else why I would need so badly to go."

Eric rose slowly from the cot and walked to the balcony door. He stood silently staring at the empty alley behind the house. "That argument leaves me no rebuttal." He spoke softly. "If your father gives his permission I will take you with me."

"Oh thank you, Eric!" She jumped up from the cot and ran to where he was standing, nearly grabbing him but recapturing her composure just in time. "I'll speak to my father just before the evening meal and I am sure he will give his permission before supper."

CHAPTER VIII

It was as Milcah said it would be, and after extensively assuring her father that he would do everything in his power to see to his daughter's safety and honor, Eric and Milcah, with a well-provisioned donkey, set out the next morning through the nearly empty streets toward the north gate. The sun was just catching the tops of the white, weather bleached houses and most of the city was still asleep.

The listless Roman soldiers made no attempt to detain traffic going out of the city. The morning desert air smelled good and Eric found himself in excellent spirits. Even though he had originally opposed the idea, he was glad to have Milcah with him. Not only did he feel that she would be of great assistance to him, but he found that he just plain liked having her around.

They would first have to make a stop at Edh Dhahriye to pay their respects, as promised, to Ishmael before continuing north. They should arrive at the synagogue by late afternoon, which meant they had a whole day of travel ahead of them.

Eric was on an unbelievable natural high. An old song from his childhood, called "On The Street Where You Live," kept running through his brain. It made no sense at all except that the song, as he remembered it, was full of anticipation because someone was near at hand and, at any second, something magical could happen. In some way, he was feeling that same sense of anticipation walking along this desert road, just knowing that somewhere, probably within a hundred mile radius, Jesus Christ was sleeping, having breakfast, or doing what he referred to as "his father's work."

My God, the thought struck him, if I do find him, what would I ever say? How will I talk to him? Will he know who I am? Will he know about the future? The questions and fantasies kept cycling through Eric's mind with endless variations.

For the first time since his "arrival," he also gave some thought to going back. Would his body revert back to its normal condition? What would be the most indisputable piece of evidence he could take back with him to document his journey? Would matter transmit forward in time, using the same set old conditions that had brought him backwards? How is Wendell surviving all those closed door meetings he must be having at Cal Tech with all of N.A.S.A.'s top brass? Once again, a wave of guilt swept over him as he felt a sense of the betrayal he had inflicted upon his old friend.

On and on it went, one thought leading to another. Milcah must have been having somewhat parallel thoughts because when she finally broke the silence between them it was to ask, "Eric, what is the world like in the time and place you come from?"

"Oddly enough," Eric said, after having thought about it for a moment, "although man has accomplished great things, many things about the world are exactly the same as they are today."

"How do you mean that?" she asked.

"Well, in my world, man has still not learned to live without wars. The same greed and lust for power that drives men today is still in the world 2000 years from now. People still persecute other people because they are different in color, religion, philosophy, or political beliefs. Only, in the future the instruments of destruction are much more sophisticated.

"You see, Milcah, the world went on for a long time pretty much the way it is today. Man finally explored and made settlements in most of the world after he found out it was a globe, like I told you, and the people of the earth came to number in the billions. It's difficult to say when it all started, but only a hundred years or so before I was born the world went through what was to be called the 'Industrial Revolution'. Men began to invent and build all sorts of machines to make life easier and better for himself. Where

90

he once had to pick the seeds out of cotton by hand he built a machine that could do it much faster. He built a boat that would run by a steam machine and he no longer had to depend on the wind or oars. Technology virtually exploded over the next hundred years in all things from medicine to architecture. We built machines that wash your clothes, look inside your body, let you talk to and see people thousands of kilometers away, fly you around the world in a matter of hours. We even sent men to the moon. But something happened when I was only a very young child that would never let the world be the same again. There was a great global conflict, where virtually all the nations of the world were engaged in a war that lasted over five years. It was during that war that man harnessed a source of energy, which could be used for destroying all life on this planet.

"Well, some forty years later, or up until the time I came here, man had still not used that weapon in war again. However, by that time, those weapons now existed by the thousands and if they were ever used they reduce the earth to a cinder. The world, for as long as I can remember, has lived with the threat of this horrible possibility. The thing that frightens most thinking people in the world I come from is that man, with all of his progress in what we call technology, has made absolutely no progress in his ability or willingness to develop a peaceful co-existence with his fellow man. The world waits in fear and wonders how long one can exist in the eye of a hurricane, with two mighty nations possessing most of the weapons and playing with the rest of the nations of the world like chess men, wooing them to their particular beliefs.

Then one of the superpowers collapsed and, for a while, the world breathed a false sigh of relief, for unknown to most of the world, an even more menacing monster was secretly growing in strength based upon a twisted version of Islam. They are religious fanatics whose sole dedication is to kill everyone not accepting their views. Their first priorities appear to be Israelis and the rest of the Western culture not agreeing with their fundamentalist beliefs."

As Eric paused a moment to reflect on his own thoughts, Milcah questioned, "Eric, how is it possible that men who are wise enough to build machines that will fly to the moon could also be foolish enough to build machines that they live in fear of?" "It seems, my dear child, that there is a great deal of difference between intelligence and wisdom."

"Huh?" Milcah flipped, changing the subject. "Why do you call me child?" "Well," he stuttered a little, "it's only an expression, and there is certainly nothing child-like about you. However, I am seventeen years older than you, so, biologically, I am old enough to be your father." "Age differences like that are for girls, not women. Besides, from what you have told me, I am still nearly two thousand years older than you, so your seventeen years pale somewhat in significance, wouldn't you say?"

"What I say is, I would love to have had you on our debating team at M.I.T."

"There you go," she said. "Every time I get close to understanding something, you interject something else of which I have never heard!"

"It was only a bad joke," Eric smiled. "What it meant was that your point about our ages was well made."

A faint smile of satisfaction turned up the corners of Milcah's mouth as they continued down the road mostly in silence, broken occasionally by the questions that kept popping into Milcah's head.

The day passed uneventfully. The weather was as perfect for traveling as the Judean desert could offer. They had covered over ten kilometers by noon in spite of some intermittent resistance on the part of their ass, whom Milcah had named "Augustus." Once they passed a caravan of five small carts headed towards Beersheba but the dialog they exchanged was limited to polite greetings as they each continued on their respective ways.

About two kilometers further on they came to a building surrounded by a wall, with a courtyard in front. From his directions, this had to be the synagogue where Ishmael was serving his apprenticeship. It would be good to see him again and Eric was especially interested in the process of the scrolls actually being written and hoped that a tour, of sorts, could be arranged. As they neared the gate they could see four horses tied to a hitching post. They appeared to be Roman cavalry but they thought nothing of it as they tied Augustus next to his larger companions. They passed through the open gate and knocked on the large cedar door that was the main entrance. A moment later, a bearded young man in his late twenties appeared and bade them to enter. They came into a rather large room that contained a single bench. The temperature inside was at least ten degrees cooler because of the two-foot thick walls.

After exchanging greetings with the young man they asked if they could see their friend, Ishmael. Eric thought he detected just the slightest change of expression in his eyes as he excused himself, explaining that he would return shortly. He left through the only other door in the room, closing it behind him.

They waited in silence for no more than a minute before the door reopened and, to their surprise, the room filled with people. The young man who greeted them entered first, followed by an older priest with a very large beard which gave him a look of authority. Next there were four Roman soldiers (Eric remembered the horses), followed by Ishmael and another small, rather homely man in his mid-thirties, with wiry red hair and an unmistakable look of intelligence in his eyes. Ishmael looked ill at ease, and Eric felt a corresponding uneasy felling welling up in him.

The older priest spoke first: "Is this the man of whom you spoke?" He directed the question to Ishmael.

"Yes, Rabbi," Ishmael sounded embarrassed, and his eyes would not meet Eric's, "but I do not feel..."

"What you feel will best be determined by someone more qualified to judge!" the priest interrupted.

Ishmael lapsed into obedient silence as the priest addressed Eric. "Our young apprentice has told us of your journey together and that you performed many signs and showed a great deal of interest in a man called Jesus." He paused for a reaction, but Eric said nothing; so the priest continued. "We have a man with us here today," nodding toward the homely, red haired man, "who is not a priest, yet deals with matters of this sort on our behalf."

"Matters of what sort?" Eric asked.

"Soothsayers, workers of magic, as well as those who would follow preachers of blasphemy. But then, if you are not guilty of any of these he will be equally quick to determine your innocence."

With that, the two priests left the room taking Ishmael with them, but leaving the little man and the four soldiers in the room with Eric and Milcah.

After an appropriate period of silence and a lengthy visual survey of his suspects (tactics practiced by all interrogators, and designed to intimidate), the red haired little man approached Eric with the arrogance of a small bully backed up by large friends.

"The young apprentice was quite impressed by some of the acts you performed," he began in a rather high pitched voice that had a haughty ring to it. "So impressed, in fact, that at first he thought you might be the Messiah."

He turned his back on Eric and walked a step or two away. Then he wheeled abruptly and asked, "Are you the Messiah?"

Eric, unruffled by the theatrics, answered calmly. "What did Ishmael say my answer was to that question?"

"You saw the look in the boy's eyes. Obviously he is captivated by you and, of course, he confirms your denial of any association with this rabble rouser or his organization. He said that you claimed to be merely a merchant from a place called Britannica, laden with expensive toys."

Eric really didn't like the direction this inquisition was taking, so he decided to go on the attack and become indignant.

"And just who are you, sir, to question me in this manner? I am not used to being treated like a criminal. So either accuse me of a crime or I am going to take my friend and leave this place right now."

The little man was unimpressed. And why not? He was still two thousand years removed from a peculiarity in Western law that would come to be known as civil rights.

"My name is Saul. You will leave when and if I choose to release you."

He delivered the statement with the pomposity of a celebrity, expecting his unenlightened audience to respond with some sort of recognition.

The statement worked. But in his wildest dreams Saul could not have imagined the reaction he triggered. All of a sudden a bell went off in Eric's head... something became connected that he had been trying to put together since the whole group came into the room. Saul...Saul... could it be? He certainly fit the physical description. And his persecution of Jesus' followers prior to his conversion was well known. Could this really be him, the zealous Pharisee appointed to do the work unbefitting the priesthood? The one that history would refer to as the "great lion of God?" Somehow, he was sure that the man there before him was the one who would come to be known as Paul, and who, in later times, the Christian world would know as Saint Paul.

Was he actually face to face with the most devout spokesman for Christianity of all time? If it were true this, then, would be the man who would write more books (through his letters) of the New Testament then any other author in the Bible. The rebel, not of the original twelve, but the one appointed by Jesus to fill the vacancy created by Judas Iscariot.

That is who he would be someday, but for now they confronted the immediate problem of being detained by an arrogant, self-righteous little jerk, out to impress these priests with his interrogative skills.

Regardless of his instinctive feelings, Eric knew that if he could only confirm a few more known facts about this man he would have the answer. He decided to try a different approach.

"Forgive me, it was most assuredly not my intention to offend you. I will be happy to cooperate in clearing up whatever confusion may have been caused by the young man's over-active imagination."

"A wise decision," Saul smirked, "One that will save us both a great deal of time and you, perhaps, a great deal of discomfort."

"First, though, may I ask you, sir, if you are not the one from Tarsus, the son of a Pharisee and also a Roman citizen, an honor which was bestowed upon you?"

Saul gave Eric a look of curious surprise. "Do I know you?" he asked.

"And did you not study the scriptures in Jerusalem under the most honored Rabbi Gamaliel?" Eric continued.

"What you are saying is not a secret, but how is it that you know of these things?"

"May I ask you if..."

"No! You may not!" Saul shouted at him. "I think you've lost track of the fact that I'm the one asking the questions!" His voice was shaking with anger at himself for allowing the other to control the conversation.

"Perhaps we've already talked enough," he said, his voice once more under control. "Let's have a look at some of these 'wondrous toys' you carry with you." His hand moved toward the strap of Eric's backpack, but Eric pushed it away with the swift reaction of a fighter blocking a left hook. This brought a renewed flush of anger to Saul's face.

The soldiers, who had been only mute, bored bystanders to now, immediately sprang into a ready position with their spears. It was as if the pin had been pulled on a hand grenade, and in an instant the room was filled with explosive tension. Eric knew that he had to do something, and do it fast, to calm the situation down. He also knew that Saul would not be denied his inspection, and that was something he simply could not allow to happen.

"Forgive me," he said in the calmest voice he could muster, "that was a conditioned reflex. As my very livelihood is contained in this pack I tend to be over zealous in protecting it. Please allow me to display the contents for you."

He hoped he didn't sound as nervous as he felt, jabbering something in an attempt to defuse the tension while he took off his pack and set it on the floor. He reached inside and felt around the various objects until he came across the one thing he had hoped he would never have occasion to use. It was a small cartridge air gun which held a miniature magazine of fifty needles. The tiny missiles were less than a quarter of an inch in length and dissolved upon impact; yet each could render a two-hundred pound man unconscious almost instantly and the effects would last for nearly half an hour.

"The first little toy is the favorite of the Syrian Court," Eric said, sounding like a T.V. pitchman. "It is used in playing a game called 'All fall down.'" As he rambled on he turned slowly, firing a nearly silent missile into each guard, in the two seconds it took him to get to the fourth guard the first to be hit was buckling, and one at a time they dropped to the floor, their spears clanging against the stones in a glissando of anvil harmony.

It all happened so quickly that after the last soldier slumped to the floor Saul just stood there staring down at them in bewilderment.

"Please," Eric broke the silence, "it is imperative that we continue on our journey. We mean no harm to you or anyone else."

"What then have you done to these men?" Saul found his voice.

"They are only sleeping and will awaken shortly. I really would like to talk to you at great length about the man you have yet to become but, for now, we really must be on our way."

"I don't know who, or what, you are with your magic and your talk of what I am to become, but you shall not walk by me, you will have to walk over me." He defiantly positioned himself between them and the door.

What a gutsy little guy, Eric thought. I'm a head taller and sixty pounds heavier than him, he's just watched me put away four soldiers, and still he's ready to try to stop me from leaving. No wonder Jesus would someday choose him to fight for his side.

"I'm sincerely sorry that we could not have met under different circumstances," Eric said. "We all must do what we have to do. You will deal with your own destiny in a short while, on the road to Damascus. But as for me and the woman, we have a destiny that must be dealt with now, and we cannot allow anything to interfere with it. Try to forgive me for what I must do."

With that, Eric released a fifth dart. Saul stood there for a second before his eyes rolled back in his head. Eric caught him before he hit the floor and laid him down gently.

"Quickly," he said, slipping his pack on and taking Milcah by the hand. "We must put all the distance we can between us and this place before the drug wears off."

Milcah was too confused and frightened to do anything but follow without question. They left through the door they had come in, and walked casually across the courtyard in order not to draw attention to themselves, but the yard was empty and no one saw them leaving.

Eric transferred their pack from Augustus to one of the soldiers' horses, as the little guy would only slow them down. They left with all four horses at a gallop, making sure the soldiers could not mount a pursuit when they awoke. Some distance down the road they slowed their pace as they were still several kilometers from Edh Dhahriye. They rode on in silence for some distance.

Milcah spoke first. "Is it true that those men will be all right?"

"Yes."

"They looked like they were dead."

"Only sleeping. They will waken shortly."

"I think I would be frightened to live in your world with such weapons."

"I'm glad you will not be exposed to the kinds of weapons most often used in my world. But what we must be concerned with now is what will happen when they do wake up. They will be slowed down for sure without their horses, but I think we can count on the fact that we will be hunted."

"Do you think it would have been best to have just told him about yourself?"

"I couldn't possibly have risked his reaction to that, and I'm positive that he could not have kept information of that nature to himself without revealing it to higher authorities. It's just imperative that I don't draw attention to myself."

"For a man nearly a head taller than everyone else, with pale blue eyes, speaking with an accent and riding a Roman soldier's horse, I think you stand just a modest chance of being noticed."

"I appreciate your pointing that out to me," he smiled at her. "We'll get rid of the horses before we get to Edh Dhahriye and try to join a large caravan, or just lose ourselves in the largest crowds we can, and hope that Saul and the Romans' interest in us is short lived."

"Eric, why did you speak to that man as if you knew him? What did you mean when you spoke of the 'man he will someday be?'"

Eric didn't answer right away, so Milcah continued, "How did you know so much about him? The strangest look came over your face as you were talking to him and you began speaking to him in a tone of near reverence."

"It was an encounter for which I was totally unprepared," Eric said, staring ahead, as if talking to himself. "This man Jesus who we are seeking, will appoint twelve apostles to establish his Church, but one of those twelve will betray him and in time this man we were talking to will be appointed to take the place of the one who betrayed him."

"This man? He did not seem at all favorable towards anyone who might speak well of Jesus or his followers."

"He's not, and unfortunately for us, I'm going to guess that he was – is - as dedicated in his persecution of Jesus' followers now as he will be in championing his cause later."

"So that's why you treated him with such tenderness?" Milcah spoke with understanding.

"Yes. But for right now, the less we see of Saul, the better. All he'll be thinking about us is that we humiliated him by escaping, to say nothing of stealing the Roman horses."

""Perhaps if they are humiliated they will just choose to forget it," Milcah said, with no conviction.

"Not a chance. When they tell the high priests what happened to them they're sure to connect it to some sort of demon-inspired act. They'll probably even claim it to be inspired by Jesus, so I don't think we can count on them to just write us off."

"Write us off?" she asked.

"Sorry, I did it again. It's just an expression that can be used to say 'forget about it' or 'we won't count on that.'"

"Write us off," she repeated, like a child learning a new word.

They continued on for another hour or more just engaged in small talk, mostly about cultural differences, and purposely avoiding the subject of their newly acquired status as fugitives. Then Eric decided it was time to get rid of the horses. He took the saddles off and stashed them behind some rocks, then sent the horses off in a gallop with a slap on the hindquarters. He picked up the provisions pack as if it were a bag of feathers, and they started out on foot to cover the last few kilometers into Edh Dhahriye. It would be nightfall before they reached the city.

It wasn't much of a city, surely not a place where you could lose yourself in a crowd, but at least they were able to buy a donkey right away so Eric wouldn't look conspicuous carrying such a huge load besides his own backpack.

They walked down the main road leading to the market square. Eric, as usual, was gawking at the wares of the roadside vendors, still doing business by torchlight. Oils, fruits, dried fish, pottery, baskets and a variety of other things that were common, everyday objects to everyone else. But to him it was still like walking through a living history book. He smiled as he wondered how much an antique dealer in Beverly Hills would pay for the small tool engraved bronze oil lamp displayed there among the many others.

Milcah touched his arm and nodded down the road to a place where some Roman soldiers where watching a flurry of activity. His first reaction was to turn and head in another direction. Then it occurred to him that they couldn't possibly be looking for them; there was no such thing as a communications system that could carry an alarm about them. He wondered when carrier pigeons were first used.

Anyway, he was sure that the few soldiers at the synagogue were not prepared to send messages. He nodded reassuringly to Milcah and pulled the hood of his robe over his head.

"Let's go see what's going on," he said, trying to sound confident.

There seemed to be a great deal of bargaining and negotiations going on. From what Milcah could find out by milling though the crowd, a trading caravan had stopped for the night and would leave at first morning light. She also learned that there was a very important man who was traveling with it. His name was Ben Yaier, and he was said to be the one who schools the royal court in all matters of learning.

"They were saying that Herod himself goes to him on matters that only the wisest of men would know," she repeated, with a certain awe-struck tone in her voice.

"Do you know where the caravan is going?" he asked.

"To Jerusalem, then to the sea at Caesarea."

"Can we make arrangements to travel with it? We would be much less conspicuous than traveling alone."

"For a fee we can travel with the main caravan, as they offer protection from thieves and road bandits. Or we can travel with the group that lags half a kilometer behind and does not pay, but feels safer being close to a large group."

"We pay," he said.

He gave her some silver shekels, duplicates he had made of the Phoenician type minted in Tyre between 126 B.C. and 65 A.D. She would make the arrangements with the caravan master and meet him back at the open-front eating house they were standing in front of.

When Milcah left, Eric went over to a table that held several large tubs and urns. An unkempt elderly woman sat on a stool, plucking a chicken. She ignored him as he stood watching her. The faintest hint of a smile crossed his face as he thought, "Good grief, am I witnessing the invention of Jewish penicillin?"

After removing a final pin feather she grunted at him in a broken Aramaic equivalent of "Wharta ya want?"

"Just some of that," he pointed to an urn that contained something hot, and hoped it wasn't dishwater.

The old woman poured him a mug of what turned out to be hot lemon water, and sprinkled it generously with cinnamon. He seated himself on a bench at a long table that overlooked the street and watched the passersby; over half of them stepped into a mud puddle where someone had emptied a large kettle of water. At least he didn't feel as self-conscious with the mug in his hand.

Milcah soon returned and announced that all had gone well. They each had a bowl of hot porridge with ample helpings of bread and cheese. After their evening meal they agreed that staying at an inn would make them too easy to trace, so they decided to find someplace to unroll their bedrolls, get a good night's sleep, and leave at dawn with the caravan. They found a place next to a small shed, and went to sleep, knowing that their lives, from that day on, would never be the same.

CHAPTER IX

The morning broke bright and clear. The smell of camels and a variety of other livestock was distinct, but not offensive. Eric was rubbing the night's cold out of his bones to get his circulation going as Milcah gathered up their bedrolls to be tied onto the newly purchased donkey. This one she named Claudius. She seemed determined to name every ass in Judeah after one Caesar or the other. Momentarily forgetting about the extraordinary density of Eric's pack, she grabbed it as she would her own, and was instantly stunned to realize that she would have had better luck picking up the donkey. She glanced up to see Eric smiling at her.

"I still don't believe it," she said, smiling and shaking her head. "Neither do I," he said, as he easily slung it onto his back.

They chewed on some dried meat as they walked towards the area where the caravan was preparing to leave. Eric bought some fresh fruit from a street vendor while Milcah filled the goatskin pouches at the well.

The activity around the carts and wagons appeared confused and unorganized, and there seemed to be more orders being shouted at subordinates than there were subordinates carrying out orders, as everyone made their last minute preparations for the journey.

Making their way down the line, they came to a narrow aisle between a shroud-covered wagon and a cart loaded with a pyramid of barrels that some men were cinching down. Some people coming from the other direction excused themselves as both parties passed in the small space between the two wagons.

Suddenly, like a shot ringing out, a line snapped and the barrel on top dropped down, sending the one on the outside shooting out toward Eric and the others.

With the reaction of a hockey goalie, Eric's hand shot up and stopped the barrel and, in the same motion, lowered it gently to the ground. Three men came running around from the other side of the cart to survey the damage, far more concerned for the safety of the keg and its contents than for anyone who might have been injured in the mishap.

In the confusion, Eric turned to see if Milcah and the others around them were all right. No one was hurt or, for that matter, even seemed very concerned about the incident except for one old man with steel blue eyes who was staring at Eric. These were the first blue eyes he had seen since he arrived.

Eric broke eye contact with the old man, grabbed Milcah's hand, and led her away, not wishing to be connected with any incident that might cause someone to recall them to inquiring Roman soldiers.

As Eric and Milcah continued down the line of the caravan the old man with blue eyes asked the young man next to him," There are four men lifting our keg of wine back onto the cart. How much do you think it weights?"

"Probably close to three talents," the young man replied (this would have amounted to about 225 pounds). He didn't know the real reason for the question, since everything had happened so fast and he hadn't been in a position to see what Eric had done. "Excuse me, master, but it was you who gave us most of the ratios between liquids and solids. Why is it you ask me such an elementary question?"

"It's not that often that I am presented with such an opportunity to test your powers of retention, Yasmine."

A few meters down the line Eric and Milcah found a vacant place where they could fall in line when the caravan got under way.

Milcah was getting anxious. "I wish they would get started soon. Do you think they will leave on time, Eric?"

"I expect we'll get underway as soon as they restack the wine kegs down the line."

"I thought for a moment that the whole cart of wine was going to fall on us."

"It sounded worse than it was," Eric played down the incident.

A signal was shouted at the head of the caravan that started the lead wagons moving. With that delayed inertia of moving objects that Eric was never able to understand, even in modern automobile traffic, it was an exasperating length of time before the thrust of forward motion finally allowed them to move out behind the wagon preceding them.

The moment they got underway they both felt a sense of relief. Within a few moments they passed the outskirts of the city and the caravan began to stretch out in spite of the efforts of prodders, mounted on camels, who shouted at the members of the train to close their ranks.

They expected to arrive in Hebron around mid-day. Eric knew that Masada and the Dead Sea lay only about fifteen miles to the east. It seemed so near and yet so far. He found himself wishing he could just be a tourist and catch an air-conditioned bus over to the sights and maybe munch a box lunch on the way. But in the meantime, the thrill of being where he was, and seeing the things he was seeing, had not diminished. He still didn't want to pinch himself, lest he wake up from this incredible dream.

They had traveled nearly ten kilometers and already entered the foothills south of Hebron. Eric was plodding along leading Claudius when Milcah touched his arm without saying anything, staring with concern at a cloud of dust approaching from the south.

A quick glance told Eric that it was a column of Roman cavalry closing at full gallop. He quickly rejected his first reaction, which was to run; the terrain was still too flat for them to leave the caravan without being observed and certainly overtaken.

He squeezed Milcah's hand and attempted to reassure her. "They're probably not after us. But just in case they are, they'll be looking for a couple traveling together. We're going to take a few risks now," he said, with his most reassuring smile. "Just remember, I'll always be very near you." With that he took her hand and moved ahead to the largest wagon in the caravan, the same one where the incident of the falling wine keg took place. Eric pushed back the curtain and hoisted Milcah up into a well-appointed compartment.

The surprised occupants were Ben Yaier and his manservant, Yasmine. Yasmine immediately demanded to know the meaning of their intrusion. To add authority to his demand, he hastened to ask if they were aware of whose privacy they had invaded. He then demanded an immediate withdrawal, coupled with rambling threats if they failed to comply. He was silenced by the raising of, Ben Yaier's hand.

"Perhaps our guests would like to offer some sort of explanation for their unsolicited visit." He spoke softly.

"Please sir," Eric said, glancing back at the road where the Roman soldiers were now close enough to be distinguishable, "my wife is suffering from female problems and is unable to walk any further. If you would please let her rest for just a short while we would be very grateful and would pay any amount you might specify."

"Absolutely not," Yasmine began. "You might at least have asked before just..."

Again, Ben Yaier raised his hand and Yasmine fell silent.

"Not knowing the nature of the woman's problems," the old man responded, "perhaps there was not time to request permission. We have ample room to accommodate another person, as long as the arrangement is only temporary. Yasmine, would you see to making the woman as comfortable as possible? As for me, I have a need to stretch my legs and I think I should like to walk for a while. I wonder, sir," he addressed Eric, "if you would introduce your wife and yourself and then assist me down from this wagon so that I might walk with you for a spell."

Yasmine, obviously pleased with the way his master handled the situation, assisted him to the boarding step where Eric helped lower him to the ground after introducing Milcah and himself.

By now, the column of soldiers had caught up with the rear of the caravan, where people were pointing at them. Ben Yaier caught Eric's concerned glance in that direction.

"Has your wife been ill very long?" he asked Eric.

"No, it seemed to come on her suddenly."

"Could it be that she is with child?"

"Oh, no, nothing like that," he was quick to reassure.

"Well then, I wonder what has come over her." His blue eyes locked with Eric's and they both silently acknowledged that they were playing a game of sorts.

"I do indeed have a problem," Eric began, "and I know that you know that I haven't been entirely honest with you. But if you could find it within yourself to help me I can assure you that you won't regret it."

As he said this, the officer at the head of the Roman column, which consisted of sixteen horsemen, thundered by to the head of the caravan, where he barked out orders, which brought it to a halt.

"I wonder what that's all about," Ben Yaier asked of Eric.

"I have no idea," he replied, with no conviction.

Within moments soldiers had spread themselves along the length of the caravan, while five of them, led by the officer, proceeded down the caravan one wagon at a time, questioning the people and methodically searching their wagons.

Ben Yaier watched the concern on Eric's face grow as the soldiers grew closer.

When they arrived at Ben Yaier's wagon the captain put aside his arrogance and greeted the scholar politely, begging forgiveness for any inconvenience the delay was causing. He told him that his presence in the caravan was known to the troops, and his safe conduct would be assured against the likes of any fanatic rebel, such as the one they were searching for, a coward who, only yesterday, had ambushed Roman soldiers with a sneak attack.

The officer instructed his men not to inspect Ben Yaier's wagon. The old man thanked him for his courtesy and, with one of the soldiers helping him, climbed back into his compartment and closed the drapes.

With Ben Yaier gone, the officer turned his attention to Eric. He stared down at him from his horse for a few seconds, and then made a quick hand motion that signaled several soldiers to surround Eric with drawn swords.

"You fit the description of the man we are looking for! Identify yourself and say where you've hidden the woman!"

Eric stood frozen, not knowing what to do. Should he surrender peacefully and hope that someone would understand and believe him? Should he go for the Teledyne-developed phaser in his pack that could level everything in its path? Or should he count on the superhuman strength he now possessed? Killing was not part of his nature, and a thrust fist that before this journey contained only ordinary power might now, even with curtailed effort, prove fatal. A few soldiers, maybe, but this was sixteen! Even with what he assumed was an extremely dense molecular structure to his skin he didn't know if a sword or arrow would penetrate it, and now, certainly, did not seem like the time or place to test theory. But still...what to do?

"I'm not going to ask you again," the officer barked, his patience obviously gone. "Tell me your name and business... now!"

Eric felt that his arrest would mean the end of what he had started out to do. Forced into a decision, with no alternatives left, he chose to make some sort of fight of it in spite of the lousy odds, heightened by his self-imposed restrictions against risking a fatal injury to any of his opponents.

"Take him!" came the order.

Eric crouched and prepared to resist, but in that same split second a voice came from within the wagon: "Captain. The safe passage you have granted to me, is that not to include my man servant and other members of my party?"

The officer seemed somewhat shocked, almost disappointed.

"This man is a member of your party?"

"He is," Ben Yaier replied with complete composure.

"Why then, sir, didn't the fool speak up and tell us that?"

"His duties mostly require a strong back, Captain. Quickness in responding to any situation is something that cannot be expected of him. A condition which, I'm sure, is enhanced when he is confused and frightened by the sight of Roman steel."

The officer almost reluctantly motioned for his men to withdraw.

"By your leave, sir. But until we catch this criminal we are seeking I would recommend that you keep this one," nodding at Eric, "under close observation, as he fits exactly the description of the fugitive we seek."

"I will heed your advice. And again, let me express my gratitude for your courtesy and efficiency," Ben Yaier gilded the lily.

The officer saluted and acknowledged the compliment with a nod of his head. He then turned his mount down the line to continue the search.

For the first time, Eric was aware of the sweat that had formed on the palms of his hands. He breathed a visible sigh of relief.

"I don't know what caused you to do that, and right at this moment I don't really care, but I assure you, I'll be eternally grateful, Ben Yaier."

"Whatever modest degree of success I have obtained as an instructor and advisor to the king would not have been possible without a certain flare for judging character."

"I'll not disappoint your judgment," Eric assured him.

"I hope not, young man. But understand, it was not an act of pure charity. Before the soldiers arrived you committed yourself to complete honesty in return for my help. So, when the soldiers leave I will have you complete your end of the bargain."

"Is there anything in particular you would like to discuss?"

"I have conducted many experiments and written several scrolls on the subject of leverage, but the way you stopped the forward motion of that wine keg this morning, and then lowered it to the ground, went far beyond any of the laws I have been able to establish. This, then, is what we will speak about."

Eric nodded in agreement without saying a word. He knew he could not double talk his way around this wise old scholar, and why should he? Hadn't he gone out on a limb for them, although they were complete strangers? He took a risk without hesitating, and it could cost him dearly if the Romans ever found out that he had lied. It is doubtful that even his position at court could protect him. After all, Herod's throne served only as a puppet government; real authority was in the hands of Rome.

In fact, the more Eric thought about it, the greater the significance of Ben Yaier's action became. What manner of man would take such a risk to help strangers, especially knowing that they possibly had committed an act of violence?

Yes sir! Eric thought. No ordinary man, this. He held nothing back in order to help us, and I will hold nothing back from him. The credibility between the two was established with the solidarity of lifelong friends.

"You shall know whatever it is you want to know," Eric said.

"Good," Ben Yaier smiled. "Then perhaps you will also arrange an introduction to the weaver who supplied the cloth for your garment."

Eric smiled back at him, his smile acknowledging their bond and also complimenting Ben Yaier on his awareness.

"We will speak at your convenience," Eric said as he walked toward the back of the wagon where he had tied Claudius prior to thrusting Milcah into Ben Yaier's wagon. He gave him some water and adjusted the pack straps, then fidgeted as he watched the soldiers slowly finish searching the caravan.

When they had satisfied themselves with the last wagon, the officer and two of his men galloped back to Ben Yaier's. Hearing the horses pull up outside, he opened the drape.

"We are taking our leave now, sir. Is there any message you would like us to carry on ahead of you to Jerusalem?"

"None thank you. Upon my arrival I will speak personally to Favious and compliment him on the professionalism of his officers. By what name may I mention you specifically?"

Damn! He doesn't miss a trick, Eric thought.

'You are too kind, sir, but that will not be necessary. My name is Salvador Fanini and my only wish is to provide for your safely."

Hah! Eric murmured to himself. You could have provided for his safety without telling him your name.

"It is very reassuring to know that you and your men are near at hand, Captain Fanini." He spoke his name clearly so the Roman would be confident that a favorable report of him would reach the ears of the Commander of the Seventh legion.

"Have a comfortable journey." He turned his mount to return to the head of his column, but took the time to give Eric a final long, cold stare that seemed to promise "another time."

When the soldiers were well down the road and the caravan had resumed its progress, Eric stuck his head into Ben Yaier's wagon. "Your hospitality has been wonderful, but I feel sure we have overstayed our welcome. Allow me to help you down, Milcah." He extended his hand.

"On the contrary," Ben Yaier touched Milcah's shoulder so she would remain seated, "with one as charming as this, welcomes are not so easily worn out. Besides, I thought Captain what's-his-name would never leave. I have been waiting quite impatiently for our little talk. So, if you don't mind, Milcah can remain here and I will join you for some exercise."

"The honor would be mine," Eric said, offering his hand to the old man. "Here, let me help you down."

The two walked silently for several paces, then Ben Yaier spoke first. "I hope you don't intend to make me walk all the way to Hebron before you decide to talk to me."

"I'm sorry, it's just that I'm having trouble deciding where to begin."

"Have you given any consideration to the beginning?'

"Normally, your suggestion would leave little room for discussion, but in this case," he paused, "the beginning is a time that has not yet occurred."

"So what are you saying, that your 'beginning' will occur in the future?"

"It did."

"It did what?"

"My beginning started a long way into your future."

"You disappoint me, sir. I was expecting a candid conversation, not riddles or game playing." Ben Yaier did not raise his voice, but he was obviously displeased.

"I promised you the truth because of what you did for us, and I will hold nothing back. You and I are both men who have dedicated our lives to the effort of unraveling the laws of the universe and understand why things appear as they are, and behave as they do. What I am about to say you will not find readily acceptable, but please try to bear with me.

"My beginning was indeed in the future," Eric continued, "for that is where I have come from. I traveled backward in time from the future and arrived here only a few days ago. My mission is a peaceful and personal one. I have come only to seek out a man that I might speak to him; a man who is part of my history and your present. I would never be able to accomplish this if my identity were known. Roman soldiers now seek us because of an interrupted interrogation, but I assure you no one was harmed. I was being questioned because someone accidentally witnessed me using an instrument that they interpreted as some sort of miracle, or possessing magical powers. Whatever they thought, I could not risk a more thorough investigation." Eric paused for a quick assessment of Ben Yaier's reaction.

"The expression on your face tells me you're still not sure whether I'm a raving lunatic or not."

112

"And what manner of lunatic would you take me for if I accepted such a story without a certain amount of skepticism?"

"Your observations never seem to leave any room for argument," Eric said, trying to lighten the conversation.

"Well," the old scholar sighed, "whatever I expected when I came between you and that Centurion, it certainly wasn't this."

"There are a thousand things I would like to ask you," Eric said.

"Let me see if I understand this: A man who claims to have come from a future place in time, and who is in my debt for having saved him from a Roman arrest, and who has committed himself to telling me anything I want to know, wants to ask ME a thousand questions?"

"Again you've made your point with eloquence," Eric smiled. "My questions will wait."

"Well now," Ben Yaier began, "the only way I can begin my questioning is to proceed on the assumption that I have fully accepted your story. I don't feel I'm prepared right now to hear how you accomplished getting from tomorrow to today, or even to know the man's name that is important enough to inspire such a journey. No, I think my first question will be something simple by comparison. Let's begin with the incident with the wine keg. How did you handle the motion and weight with such ease?"

"That was not leverage," Eric said, searching for an explanation that would be understandable. "Nor was it a highly developed skill. In fact, it was a feat that I would not have been able to accomplish prior to taking my journey backward through time. Before the journey I possessed normal strength, but during the time it took to get here a change took place within my body that resulted in my acquiring extraordinary strength. I believe I can explain it, but it will require you to accept a whole new view of what we call the laws of physics; or the order of the laws of nature."

"I do believe that today is a day for accepting new things. Tell me of this new law I will be dealing with and your theory about the changes that took place within your body. But first," he hesitated, "it would go a long way toward lending credibility to the rest of our conversation if you could arrange some small demonstration of this strength of which you speak."

Eric looked at Ben Yaier and nodded slightly in agreement. He checked behind them and in all directions to make sure that no one else could see what he was about to do.

He moved a step or two and placed his hand under the back end of Ben Yaier's wagon that was bumping along ahead of them. The old man's face froze in a stare of disbelief as he watched the wagon continue on its way, but with the rear wheels a few inches off the ground. Eric sat the wagon down so gently that Milcah and Yasmine inside were unaware that anything unusual had happened.

Ben Yaier, still staring at Eric, spoke with no expression on his face. "The balance of our conversation will be void of any further skepticism. Tell me now what you think caused this phenomenon."

"I spoke of a different law of physics than you presently deal with. It teaches that all the things you see that appear to be solid in reality are not. Instead, they are made up of billions of tiny things we call atoms. These are far too small to see but they are the building blocks of molecules, which are also too small to see. All structures, organic or inorganic, are made up of these tiny particles. These bits of matter can be condensed by extreme velocity. It was theorized by a great scholar of my time that matter would increase in mass and time would actually slow down when it traveled at a velocity that approached the speed of light. In order to reverse time it was necessary to reach a speed of nearly twice the speed of light. I believe that being exposed to this velocity rearranged the molecular structure of my body. It condensed the atoms to several times their original density and resulted in this strength phenomenon that, even now, I have not yet learned to deal with."

Ben Yaier had a look of bewilderment on his face as Eric caught him staring at his hand. "Are you telling me that I am not solid?"

"You are the same as you were before we talked," Eric smiled. "What I am telling you is no cause for concern."

"The light, then, that comes from the sun, or is reflected off a piece of metal onto another object, you're saying that the speed that it travels can actually be measured?"

"Yes."

"How fast does it travel, then?"

"186,326 miles per second. A mile is equal to 0.624 kilometer."

"I'm doing my best," the old man said, "but would you please define a second and carry the equation out."

"A second is one-sixtieth part of a minute and there are sixty minutes in an hour and nearly twenty-four hours in a day, which is the amount of time it takes the earth to make one complete revolution."

"Revolution?"

"Yes. For it to make a full turn or revolution."

"Eric," Ben Yaier began after a thoughtful hesitation," you're not going to tell me that you believe the earth is spinning?"

"It's not a question of whether or not I believe it. It's a simple statement of fact."

"The sun and moon, yes, for my own eyes tell me that they are traveling around the earth. But surely, if the earth were moving we would feel it. The wind would blow us away, or we would be thrown up into the sky like drops of water from a spinning wheel."

"No, we would not fly off into space, and as for the sun revolving around the earth, that is only an illusion. Look," he said, grabbing a piece of fruit from a basket on the back of the wagon. "Imagine that basket to be the sun and this fruit is the earth. Now pretend that this," embedding a small pebble into the skin of the fruit, "is us. If we stood here on the face of the earth, and the earth turned like this," he rotated the fruit in front of the basket, "would it not give the illusion that the basket was the object that was moving?"

"Dear God," Ben Yaier whispered, "the... the earth is not the center of the universe?"

"In numbers, the earth is like a grain of sand in the desert, as the stars you behold with your eyes are only like the waves on the beach of a mighty ocean. Far beyond our vision are objects in the heavens at distances that no man can comprehend."

"For centuries," Eric continued, "man has found it necessary to believe, for the sake of his own importance, that everything in the universe revolves around the earth when, in fact, we are only one of nine planets that revolve around the sun, and the sun is only one of hundreds of billions of stars that are in our galaxy, and our galaxy is only one of billions of such galaxies in the universe."

Eric was reading the bewilderment building on Ben Yaier's face.

"It isn't fair to expose you in a few moments to the knowledge that it has taken men centuries to acquire. I suggest we postpone any further discussion until a later time."

"Finally you have said something that makes sense," the old man sighed, half exasperated, but in good humor. "I will have to ponder a great deal on the things you have told me."

"I would like to end with one last thought," Eric said. "Possibly some of the things I have told you will conflict with your religious beliefs, but I want you to know that, with all the technology and scientific advancements of my time, man is still unique in the universe. Or at least he is as far as anyone knows."

"Do you mean to tell me that you're actually going to leave at least one of my lifetime beliefs untouched?"

"I'll spare you the computer's opinion on the statistical odds pertaining to the probability of other life forms in the universe," Eric smiled.

"I'm going to guess that whoever these computer fellows are, that they are no less opinionated than some stiff-necked colleagues of mine."

"Perhaps not," Eric chuckled. "We will speak of computers later, but for now, we have already covered a great deal. Far more, in fact, than any ordinary mind would be able to deal with."

"Ordinary or not, it is having its share of trouble comprehending things. However, you may rest assured that the things you have told me will remain a secret with me. I would not risk being labeled demented and put in the care of a keeper for the rest of my days, by discussing them with anybody."

"It's really quite strange," Eric, said on a serious note, "in all my life I have only placed such confidence in one other person. I have only been here a few days and already I have confided in two."

"I am pleased that you have selected me as one," Ben Yaier said with sincerity. "Would it be fair to guess that the other is Milcah?"

Eric nodded confirmation.

"It is obvious to these old eyes from the way she looks at you that you stand very little risk of betrayal from her."

Eric looked at him with a quizzical expression.

"Oh, come now," Ben Yaier, said. "Do you mean to tell me that a man who has unlocked the secrets of the heavens has not yet learned to read a woman's eyes?"

"It has long been established that wisdom and knowledge can be total strangers," Eric conceded. "I'm afraid I've made a far more thorough study of mathematics than I have of women's eyes."

"A pity," Ben Yaier smiled. "When the cold winds blow you must take great comfort in the warmth you derive from your equations."

"I didn't say I was without emotions. Besides, Milcah is just a friend... and anyway, how can you be sure..." Eric was stumbling, somewhat out of control.

Ben Yaier smiled at him before announcing that it was well past his rest period and time for him to return to the wagon.

"We'll talk again soon, but for now I will yield to far more pleasant company," he said as Eric helped him up into the wagon and then helped Milcah down.

They walked a short distance before Milcah spoke. "That was a courageous thing he did for us. I thought for certain that our journey was going to end almost before it began. I've never been so frightened."

"We owe that wonderful old man much more than we will ever be able to repay," Eric agreed thoughtfully.

CHAPTER X

The balance of the journey into Hebron was a particularly joyous time. The immediate danger gone, Eric and Milcah took great comfort in their newly bonded alliance with Ben Yaier. As for him, he was like a child on Christmas morning, coming back time and time again with new questions for Eric.

Eric had brought with him an impressive set of 5x7 color photographs showing life and scientific accomplishment of modern times. The old man savored each one like a child opening a present, as he stared in wonder, being careful not to ask too many questions for fear it would slow down the viewing process. His mouth dropped open as he stared at the skyline of Manhattan, jets being launched from a nuclear carrier, the Grand Canyon, a 747 cruising at thirty thousand feet, the San Francisco Bay Bridge, medical photos showing X-rays with artificial and replacement parts, the atomic bomb, satellite photos of Saturn and other planets, a Los Angeles freeway interchange at 5:00 p.m., astronauts standing on the moon with the earth in the background. These, and a dozen or so others, held Ben Yaier spellbound. Unable to tear his eyes away from the miracles he was beholding, he asked Eric almost off-handedly how the artist was able to capture so much realistic detail in such small paintings. Eric smiled and reached into a side flap of his backpack. Still unnoticed by Ben Yaier, who was totally preoccupied, he brought out the camera and snapped his picture. The old scholar looked up at the click of the shutter and saw the strange black box in Eric's hand.

"Well now, what sort of miracles are contained in there?" he asked.

Almost as if to answer his question, the camera made a slight whirring noise and a small flat sheet appeared. Eric pulled it from the camera and held it a few seconds until it came up to full color, then handed it to Ben Yaier.

The old man started to speak, but couldn't. He kept looking at Eric and then back at the photograph. He looked like he wanted to yell 'help!', but nothing came out. It was the first time Eric had seen this brilliant mind temporarily lose composure.

Finally Eric spoke. "This is the process used to make those pictures you are looking at." Pointing to the lens, he attempted an explanation. "A very fast shutter inside here allows a quick flash of light to make an impression of what it sees on that film you are holding. Some chemicals are applied to develop it and, presto, you have a picture."

"Presto?"

"Well, that may be a slight oversimplification," Eric admitted.

"I swear, my boy, I believe that if you turned that ox over there into a camel you would say 'Presto', as if it were an everyday occurrence.

"A poet once wrote that only God can make a tree," Eric grinned.

"I take it from that, then, that there are certain limitations to the accomplishments of man?"

"Man will do what seems to be wondrous things with his technology, but will grow little, or not at all, in the areas of tolerance, love, or understanding of his fellow man. Greed and a lust for power rule in the world of tomorrow just as they do today."

"That is truly sad and frightening," Ben Yaier sighed. "Would it not have been better for man to have devoted more energy toward the understanding of one another and less toward building what you call a bomb?"

"Unfortunately, my friend, people like you and I don't run the world and we can do little to change it. That will be up to a higher authority."

"Are you speaking of divine intervention?" Ben Yaier asked.

"Yes."

"I am not as studied in the scrolls as I should be, but many Rabbis and scholars believe that very soon now the Messiah will make his appearance and establish himself as our King." He paused thoughtfully, and then added," However, from what you have told me about the future, it appears that his reign of righteousness will be only temporary."

"History tells us that many people of today are expecting all the wrong things of this Messiah."

"Eric," Ben Yaier said while stroking his beard," when we first met, you said that you had come to seek out someone. Would it be fair to guess that the one you seek is the expected Messiah?"

"As usual, your guesses are more accurate than most people's facts," Eric responded.

"Then he really does appear?"

"Many people believe he did."

"Amazing," Ben Yaier said.

"That you went to all the trouble you did to get here at this time, whereas all I had to do was exit my mother's womb when I did and, 'Presto', here we are together! Did it ever occur to you, Eric, that you do things the hard way?"

The two men looked at each other and broke out in laughter.

Milcah came up from behind them and wanted to know the joke she had missed.

"It had to do with different ways to skin a cat," Eric told her through his laughter.

Milcah made a face of disapproval and said she was glad she was spared the details.

"No, no," Eric stated," that's just another expression. We weren't really talking about skinning...Never mind, I'll explain later. You've been gone a long time."

"I've been talking to some women a few places back who have made this trip several times before, and they tell me that very soon now we'll be coming to a spring that forms a pool, and the caravan always stops there for a while." She was truly excited over the prospect of washing off some desert sand and perhaps doing a bit of laundry.

In less than half an hour, the caravan halted near the oasis. Many of the women and children started immediately for the pool hidden behind some rocks, about a hundred meters off the road. Eric and Milcah decided to wait until the crowd cleared out, while Ben Yaier announced that he was going to use the opportunity to enjoy a quiet nap in a wagon that wasn't bouncing over rocks.

They spend the next half hour chatting with various people in the caravan, with Milcah doing most of the talking. To minimize the chance of Eric's creating indelible memories due to grammatical errors and mispronounced words, she explained that he was suffering from a temporary throat infection.

When they saw most of the crowd coming back, Eric and Milcah headed up the path toward the pool. A narrow entrance between two large boulders revealed a tiny world totally out of place in this arid, hostile environment. A small pool, its clarity disturbed by the invasion of bathers, was nevertheless a beautiful sight to behold. At one end a small artesian spring fed the pool and gave the water the appearance of being boiled. Clumps of green grass and weeds grew near the water's edge along with a few tall scrub bushes and a slippery moss, which clung to most of the rocks.

Only a mother and two of her children remained in the pool. The woman was pounding her family's laundry with a rock while the children busied themselves with toy boats that they had fashioned from twigs. Engaged in their naval maneuvers, they hardly noticed as Eric and Milcah kicked off their sandals and entered the pool.

They splashed for a moment or two, savoring the cool water. Then Milcah found a large rock and proceeded to do their laundry, lest the caravan get underway on short notice.

Eric could feel a current tugging at him, and he let it pull him thirty meters or more to where a waterfall spilled into another pond about five meters below.

He couldn't resist. He turned to Milcah and called for help as he rode the falls over the slippery rocks and splashed into the pool below. Milcah instantly dropped her rock and swam and clawed her way through the pond to the place where Eric had disappeared. She braced herself between the two rocks where the water rushed through and, looking down, saw Eric floating on his back, wearing a large grin and spurting water out of his mouth.

"Eric Corbett, I hate you!" she said, shaking her fist at him.

He answered with another spout and an even broader grin.

"I'm going to gather some burrs for you laundry," she said.

"Now don't go away mad," Eric yelled at her. "If I have to spend the rest of the journey in a robe full of burrs it will probably ruin my whole lovable disposition."

"Maybe it will improve your sense of humor," she said, obviously cooling down.

"Come on down," he said. "The water is much nicer down here."

"It's the same water that was up here."

"No, no. Once it leaves there it becomes entirely different."

"Uh huh."

"Come on," he urged.

"It's too far," she complained.

"Come on. Life isn't worth living without an occasional risk."

She closed her eyes, took a deep breath, and released her grip on the rocks, allowing the current to sweep her over. She let out a slight squeal just before she plunged into the water, nearly landing on Eric.

As she came to the surface she looked at Eric for a moment, then moved closer to him, stopping only inches away. With a sudden move, she kissed him, taking him by surprise.

"Now that's what I call taking a risk," she said.

"Why do you say it's taking a risk?"

"What greater risk can a woman take than one that could invite rejection?"

Eric stood up in the pool and put his hands on Milcah's shoulders, drawing her close to him. She closed her eyes, and he kissed her, softly at first. Her full lips were warm and responding to his. His hands were underneath her wet robe, drawing her ever closer to him until it seemed their bodies were one. The skin on her back was smooth and soft, like a woman pampered a lifetime with milk baths and fine oils, instead of a shepherd girl. Eric had never known such desire before, but Milcah pushed away.

"I'm sorry," she said," I had no idea it would be like this."

"I don't understand," Eric said.

"I have longed for you to kiss me like that ever since you first dislodged my father's cart. It's just that I failed to count on the other emotions I am now feeling... the emotions within my body that tell me that if I do not walk away now I will surely jeopardize my relationship with God."

"Those same emotions are also within me, Milcah. I understand your concern but, please, do not be ashamed of what you are feeling, for those are God-given feelings. The sin only comes if we allow our feelings to take over before the proper time."

She gently laid her head on his chest, drawing comfort.

"I promise I will do all that I can to keep us both in good standing with God," Eric said.

A distant cry from the caravan master told them that their moment in time was over.

Eric cupped her face in his hands and kissed her again, ever so softly. Parting, he said," Come on or we'll be left behind. Sorry you're not going to have time to hunt for burrs."

With that, she jumped back and splashed him with water.

"You're a brat," she said.

"You'd better gather our washing," he said. "Otherwise, the goats won't even let us walk with them."

She scampered out of the water and started climbing to the higher pool. Her wet garment clung to her, revealing her soft, feminine curves. Watching her, his passion began to stir within him again. Stop taunting yourself, stupid, he thought to himself. Look the other way; otherwise your promise is going to be worth less than a politician's. Damn it all, why did she have to be so beautiful!

They rejoined the caravan and two hours later were within view of Hebron. Ben Yaier insisted that they both ride inside his wagon to insure safe passage through the Roman checkpoints on the outskirts of the city, and they welcomed his protection.

Inside the city there seemed to be significantly more soldiers milling about than there were in either Edh Dhahriye or Beersheba. Eric was relieved to find out from Ben Yaier that there was a large garrison stationed permanently near here, and that probably most of the soldiers were off duty. He kept hoping that the search for them would diminish, but he would have no way of knowing. Still, the troops made him very uncomfortable, and he would be glad to leave Hebron behind them.

Eric seemed to sense that even Ben Yaier was feeling somewhat tense. Had he been alone, he would have left the old scholar's wagon and taken his changes in the crowd, but if he did that it would have placed Milcah in jeopardy.

"Are we staying here over night?" Eric asked Yasmine.

"That is what I was told at the posts outside the city.'

"Halhul is only another seven kilometers, and we still have an hour of daylight left. I wonder how the caravan master would feel about moving on? Would you feel him out on my behalf, Yasmine?" Ben Yaier asked.

"Yes, master," he said, and left the wagon.

"Some of the soldiers seem to be drunk," Milcah said, peering out through a crack in the curtain.

Ben Yaier shook his head. "Pity the poor citizens of Hebron this night, for I believe that those dear Roman boys have just been paid."

"Is that bad?" Milcah asked.

"It seems, my dear, that a tour of duty in Palestine is not something that is considered a reward for meritorious service. Among Caesar's Legions, almost every soldier who has ever ran afoul of his duties is here, and does everything in his power to forget that fact on paydays."

Yasmine returned with word that the caravan would stay in Hebron overnight. Already, many members of the caravan were vying with their goods for the pay-laden purses of the soldiers.

"No matter," Ben Yaier said, sensing their uneasiness. "They've already searched the caravan, so you two just be sure to stay in the wagon, at least until after dark, and everything will be fine. We'll enjoy some dinner, and by this time tomorrow night we'll be in Bethlehem."

Bethlehem, Eric thought. It's going to be fantastic to see it as it was, or is, or whatever. Anyway, he felt better now, and would dream tonight of seeing Bethlehem tomorrow.

CHAPTER XI

Dawn found Hebron already bustling with activity. Two small boys teasing a cage full of geese soon had everyone awake. Fortunately, the geese were rescued by their irate owner. The morning also found the Roman soldiers totally absent from the area, which was reason enough to have a good day.

Eric and Milcah set out for the public bathhouse a few blocks away. Finishing first, Milcah decided to pick up some fruit from the street vendors on the way back.

A small patrol, consisting of a sergeant and four other soldiers, sat on the broken stone walls that formed the stalls of the outdoor market place, half-heartedly eating hard biscuits and wild honey. Their job was to keep the peace between the civilian population and the steam-venting soldiers, and it had been a long night. Now most of their comrades were sleeping off the effects of a vintage not known for its mellow aging. In fact, among themselves, the Hebrew wine merchants referred to it as "Military Swill."

Three of them were recalling an event of last evening, when it took all of them to subdue a two hundred pound, shovel-wielding prostitute who was intent on planting it in the skull of a piece of Caesar's property who had failed to live up to a pre-determined financial arrangement. It was one of those stories that would be embellished with each telling, and which served as an unintended testimonial to the lack of adventurous tales available to the soldiers serving in this desolate land.

The other soldier was talking to the squad leader and fidgeting with the long black woven bullwhip that one man in every squad had to carry for use in crowd control. He was on at least the sixtieth telling of his encounter with the fugitive who possessed magical powers, retracing how he was one of five people who simply fell under a spell when this tall magician pointed his demonic finger at them; although one of the guards had sworn that he was holding something in his hand.

"I tell you, Santori, it was just like waking up out of a dream. You talk about one mad Jew! This little guy that was questioning those people for the Rabbis was madder than a pregnant scorpion flipped on her back! I never saw such carryings on. I thought for sure he was going to burst every blood vessel in his body, and I almost wish he would have. These damned Jews can get more upset about that Jehovah and whoever it is he's supposed to be sending to them than you and I would if we found out we had to do another tour of duty in this god-forsaken country."

"Give it a rest, Rafius," the old, battle hardened Sergeant interrupted. "That's all you've been jabbering about since you got back. Besides, I know you all got the Captain to buy it, but don't expect me to. In seven campaigns, no man has ever had me at his feet, and I'll be damned if one could ever do it by pointing his finger at me!"

"Well, it's the truth, whether you believe me or not. And you can believe one other thing. If I ever meet up with him again he's not going to have a chance to point at me. Next time, my sword will speak first and the little Jew can talk to him later. The next time..." He stopped in the middle of a sentence that had no audience anyway, and stared down the street, squinting his eyes against the early morning sun.

It was his silence that finally got the attention of Santori. Looking up, he saw his vocal subordinated locked into an intense stare, his hand acting as a shield over his eyes.

"What the hell's interesting enough to shut you up?" the old soldier asked. Looking in the direction that the other was staring, he saw the partially silhouetted figure of a woman walking toward them down the nearly deserted street.

"It's her." He paused until she got a little closer. "By the gods, I'm sure that's her!"

"It's who?" the squad leader asked.

"The woman who was with the magician."

"Are you sure?" the Sergeant asked, looking at the woman more intently now.

Milcah had been busy inspecting the fruit she had just purchased, and looked up to notice the soldiers for the first time. Although startled, she would have regained her composure and acted as if nothing was wrong, but she knew from the way they were looking at her that something was very wrong.

Less than twenty meters separated them now as Milcah watched the rugged squad leader get to his feet, still staring at her. She could feel her heart begin to pound and wondered if they could sense her fear. For a split second she was on the verge of turning and running, but she knew that such a choice would surely invite disaster. She kept walking.

"A word with you, woman!" The soldier's gravel voice sent Milcah's heart jumping into her mouth.

"Be careful, Sergeant," the younger soldier shouted, "she may have the same powers he has!"

Now Milcah knew for certain that they had identified her, and the only instinct she had that was still fully functioning screamed at her to escape. She dropped the fruit and turned, running back up the street. The soldiers gave instant pursuit.

Milcah rounded the corner where a few street vendors were set up to catch the early morning trade, and ran smack into a merchant carrying a basket full of dried figs. Both of them sprawled in the street.

The impact of the collision, along with the bellowing profanities of the surprised merchant, focused the attention of everyone on the mishap, providing most with an early morning chuckle. The laughter was short-lived, though, vanishing immediately when the pursuing soldiers rounded the corner.

The big veteran was the first to arrive, and he reached down and grabbed Milcah by the hair, pulling her painfully to her feet. He locked his other huge arm around her waist and turned her toward the soldier who had identified her.

"Take a good look, now. Are you sure this is her?"

"That's her, all right. I may not recognize him, but I spent plenty of time watching her."

"All right, Jewess," he said, yanking her head back with his handful of hair. "Where do I find your boyfriend who knocks men down without touching them?"

"I don't know what you're talking about. Please, let me go," Milcah managed, in a trembling voice.

"Let you go? I'll let you go! All you have to do is take me to old magic finger!"

"Please," she whimpered, "I don't know who you're talking about."

"Now listen, you slut, half the Legion is looking for this friend of yours and he could be my passage out of this slime pit you Jews call home, so you're going to tell me one way or the other. The choice is yours."

"Please, I know nothing," she pleaded.

"Have it your way, woman! Hang her from that cross beam," he said, handing her to two of the soldiers and nodding toward an overhanging beam separating two stalls.

Milcah was trying to fight off panic as the two soldiers bound her wrists with their leather toga belts, hoisting her arms straight up. When they had secured her to the beam they let go, leaving her dangling with the toes of her sandals barely touching the ground. She hung there helpless as the determined squad leader approached her. She was too frightened to even feel the straps biting into her wrists.

He stood there for a moment staring at her, his breath reeking of garlic. Suddenly he reached up and gave her robe a yank, stripping her naked to her waist. Her eyes closed tightly in the shame of being exposed before strangers.

He stood there another moment, surveying her loveliness. "It's amazing," he smirked, "the things hidden by the stupid way you people dress."

By now, the crowd had grown quite large. As Santori took the whip from his subordinate he scanned the crowd for any signs of possible trouble from young radicals who might be foolhardy enough to interfere with Roman justice. Satisfied, he turned his attention back to Milcah. "Now woman, you just let me know when you're ready to take me to your friend."

With that he brought the whip down. Milcah's whole body shuddered and her scream filled the morning air, as it bit into her soft flesh, leaving an ugly red welt in its wake.

Eric was leisurely returning from the baths, still fascinated by even the smallest details of his newfound world. He had just rounded the corner when he saw the crowd and heard Milcah's scream. In that instant all reason fled and instinct took over. He didn't know what was happening, but he knew that something was terribly wrong as he charged into the crowd.

He arrived just as the soldier had his arm back to deliver a second blow. With a sweeping motion of both his arms he scattered the people in front of him like so many straws and grabbed the soldier's wrist just as it started its forward arc. The big Sergeant was yanked backwards, his wrist broken and his shoulder dislocated as he slammed to the ground with a scream of pain. With one hand, Eric grabbed the nearest soldier at the top of his leather breastplate and nearly yanked him out of his sandals. All in the same motion, he heaved him at two of the others, still too surprised to respond. The sound of the impact as all three crashed against the back wall of the market stall left no doubt in anyone's mind that none of them would be returning for a second round. They all slumped into a pile, like so many rag dolls. Years of instinctive combat training, however, brought Santori to one knee, ignoring the pain in his wrist and shoulder. He was nearly on his feet and was drawing his sword, somewhat awkwardly with his left hand. An old woman shrieked a warning and Eric turned to see the sword clearing its sheath. A quick backhand, that normally would not have amounted to much more than a slap, broke Santori's jaw; he was unconscious before he hit the ground.

Rafius stood frozen as he watched the fate of his comrades. In spite of his endless bragging about his next encounter with the tall magician he knew he had no stomach for the meeting. He was even more sure of that now, and he

131

turned to run, but he got less than three steps when he was stopped dead in his tracks by an iron kettle in his face. Rafius stumbled backwards into the circle formed by the crowd, and sprawled spread-eagle on his back, his bleeding nose pointing in a different direction than it used to. A young Jew, with an iron kettle in his hand, stepped into view and smiled at Eric.

Eric gave him a quick nod of approval but his only thoughts at the moment were of Milcah. He took a blanket from one of the merchant spectators without asking, and hurried over to where she was suspended.

"Oh, Eric," she sobbed.

"It's all right. Everything is going to be all right now." He quickly draped the blanket around her to cover her nakedness. Putting his arm around her waist he lifted her to take the weight off her wrists. He reached up and snapped the two leather belts that held her as if they were threads, and set her down.

"Can you walk?" he asked.

"I'm fine," she said, although her voice quivered as she spoke. "My pride hurts much more than my back."

"Excuse me sir," the young man, still holding the kettle, tapped Eric on the shoulder. "I have never seen a man so powerful. It was beautiful! Where did you develop such a skill?"

"I'm very grateful for your help. If that soldier had gotten away he would have had half the troops in Hebron after us right now. As it is, we'll have a short enough head start, so if you'll excuse me..."

"Wait, wait just a minute, please," the young man pleaded. "We can help you."

Eric hesitated, but said nothing.

"Now look," he was very intent as he spoke, "I don't know who you are, but I do know that you have a power unlike other men, and I just saw you use that power against Rome."

"You saw a man unwilling to watch a lady being whipped."

The young Jew drew a hidden knife and cut the leather straps from Milcah's wrists, then gave a yank as hard as he could... nothing happened.

"I just watched you break these like they were spider webs. You picked that soldier up and threw him like he was a sack of wool. Don't you see, if we knew more of these skills it would help us in our fight against Rome."

"I take no pleasure in hurting others, and wish only to be left alone. Thank you for your help." Eric started to guide Milcah away.

"Are you with the caravan?"

Eric's first reaction was to lie, but on second thought, he realized this man was now his accomplice. Besides, he felt a certain camaraderie toward him. "Yes," he answered.

"My name is Elam. I am second in command of the Zealots in Hebron. We are a resistance movement dedicated to doing everything in our power towards making the Roman invaders' occupation of our country less pleasant until the day we drive them out altogether. We will gather up these pigs you have strewn around, gag and blindfold them, and even reluctantly tend to their wounds, in a hiding place where they cannot report this incident. In due time we will release them, but by then you'll be well away from here."

"I would be very grateful for your help, as I have placed others besides myself in jeopardy. There is nothing I can give you in return except a modest amount of gold."

"We don't need your gold. We need your fighting skill!"

"I would help you if I could, but what you saw was the result of a condition that cannot be taught or duplicated and not a highly trained skill."

"What sort of condition and why can't it be duplicated?"

"I'm sorry, I don't have the answer to some of your questions, nor time for any others. Thank you for your help and any head start you could arrange for us would be most appreciated."

"The manner in which you speak tells me you are not a Jew, but it's plain that you're an enemy of Rome, so I suppose that alone entitles you to our support. Hurry! Take the woman and go back to the caravan. It should be leaving at any moment."

"Will you, or any of these people, be in any trouble?" Eric asked.

"We will send a message to the centurion that his men will be returned in two days. They may come down with reprisals later, just to save face, but on the other hand, they won't launch an all-out search for the first two days because they know it would end in failure and they would lose even more face."

Eric thanked Elam again before he and Milcah returned to the caravan, arriving just as it was getting under way.

Ben Yaier was visibly concerned when he learned what had happened, but relieved when he heard of Elam's intervention and the two-day's relief he would provide. Perhaps now they could settle down to an enjoyable journey to Jerusalem.

CHAPTER XII

It was indeed an enjoyable journey, despite making slower progress than anticipated because of the more rugged terrain they had entered, and the inevitable breakdowns that resulted. Eric, Milcah and Ben Yaier thoroughly reveled in exchanging information about the things that had separated their cultures over nearly two thousand years.

Ben Yaier spent most of the six kilometers into Halhul fascinated by Eric's quartz digital wristwatch that boasted a calculator that was far removed from the Greek Euclid Elements, a compilation and organization in thirteen sections of the accomplishments of Greek geometry. Milcah, on the other hand, was full of questions about the effects of the teachings of Jesus and the woman's role in a world of the fifth millennium.

The caravan didn't normally travel after dusk, but apparently a decision had been made to spend the night in Bethlehem rather than on the road, so they pushed on. It was after nightfall when they first caught sight of the "City of David."

Eric again felt the excitement growing in him as he looked around at the surrounding hills and wondered if any of them was where the angels had appeared to the shepherds to announce the birth of Jesus, thirty-some odd years earlier. He wondered, also, if it would be possible to locate the inn and look upon the stable where the event took place. If there were some way of locating the inn could it be that anyone there would remember the birth of a child that occurred so long ago?

Waiting impatiently for the caravan to grind to a halt, he briefly explained to Milcah the significance of the place where Jesus was born.

Ben Yaier protested only slightly, pointing out the wisdom of their remaining within the safety of his wagon until they reached Jerusalem. However, since there was no evidence of Roman activity, and with assurances from Eric and Milcah that they would do nothing to attract attention, he wished them well and bade them goodnight.

The desert sun had darkened Eric's skin, making him somewhat less conspicuous. However, they agreed that Milcah would be the one to make inquiries of the strangers they met in the streets about the location of the various inns in the city.

Bethlehem was a small but busy place. They were surprised to learn that only one inn of any significance existed, even though it was on a caravan trade route. There were, however, several other houses that offered lodging to travelers. The hospice, or inn, built during the time of David nearly a thousand years earlier, stood at the edge of the dusty square that served as a market place.

There was another caravan that was headed south also staying over in Bethlehem that night. It had arrived ahead of them, so the square was bustling with activity as the merchants noisily hawked their food and other wares. The courtyard of the old caravansary was crowded with weary travelers and their animals, bedding down for the night.

Inside, the un-hospitable innkeeper anticipated their question and told them, unasked, that there were no rooms available.

Undaunted by the man's abruptness, Milcah asked him if he, or anyone else at the inn, had been there some thirty years ago during the first Roman census.

He raised his head for the first time and, through tired looking eyes gave Eric and Milcah a disapproving look and asked to know the reason for such a seemingly ludicrous question. Milcah explained that her husband was an historian from Alexandria, doing research for the Synagogue at Caesarea. They were here attempting to confirm rumors that had to do with some unusual happenings surrounding the birth of a child at that time.

Once again the man gave them a weary scanning and grunted, "I don't know what you're talking about."

Milcah thanked him politely and they turned to leave. As they neared the door the man called, "Wait." He now spoke in a low voice. "During the time you spoke of I worked as a weaver in my father's house in Amathus, but there is a man who lives here who seems to talk of nothing but his memories of that census. Many people in the village think he's possessed, but he's really harmless and he may be willing to talk to you. His name is Silas. He lives behind his leather shop, three doors past the bakery, on the left."

"Thank you. You have been very kind," Milcah said gratefully.

The man only nodded and went back to his chores.

They quickly found the place. A heavy set woman of about forty answered their knock, holding and oil lamp. Seeing strangers, she brusquely told them that they were closed for the night, and started to close the door.

Milcah placed her hand on the door. "Wait. We were told that a man named Silas lives here, and we would like to speak to him."

"What about?" the woman demanded.

"About an event that occurred many years ago, during the census."

"Who sent you here?"

"The innkeeper directed us."

"My husband has gone to bed. He knows nothing of that time. He only made up boyhood stories." She started to close the door again.

"Please." Eric spoke for the first time. "We have traveled a long way and we must leave in the morning."

Just then a small, stooped man parted the curtains at the rear of the tiny shop. He was probably around Eric's age, but his balding head and unshaven face, that wasn't quite a beard, made him appear much older. He spoke to them from across the room in a soft voice. "What is the purpose of your inquiry?"

There was a second's pause, then Eric spoke.

"It is only curiosity on our part. I am a stranger in your country, observing points of interest and history. I had heard that some unusual events occurred during the registration, around thirty years ago. We sought only to learn if anyone remembered anything of the incident."

"We know of no such incident," the woman said, with growing tension.

"Are you a Roman?" the man asked in the same soft-spoken manner, ignoring his wife's intrusion.

"No," Eric replied. "Only a merchant from Alexandria with an interest in your history."

"It has been said that one called Saul of Tarsus travels throughout Judea, making similar inquiries, sometimes asking questions that don't pertain directly to the information he truly seeks."

"I seek nothing beyond what I have asked," Eric answered.

The man walked to the doorway and studied Eric's face for a few seconds, as if to find some assurance. Finally he told them to enter and shut the door.

"I was a boy of twelve, working here in my father's shop. It was also the year of the giant star, which I recall was the subject of much discussion. The city was teeming with activity and no hope of accommodating all the travelers who had come to register. No one in Bethlehem will ever be able to forget that year, but few will speak of it, for it was also the time when Herod's soldiers killed all the male infants in Bethlehem and the nearby districts. My own baby brother was among the victims." His voice broke slightly; the passing years still had not erased the pain and horror of that memory.

"We later learned," he continued after regaining his composure," that Herod, the father of Herod Antipas, lived in fear of a new-born child who would one day threaten his kingdom. I have often wondered through the years if that child who was born here could have been the one that Herod feared, for there was indeed something unusual about him."

"Then there was a child born here at that time?" Eric's voice was filled with anticipation. "Where? Can you tell me where the mother gave birth?"

"It was in one of the caves on the hillside, just out of town, where the local herdsmen stable their flocks."

"I thought the stable was at the inn," Eric said.

"The inn, the stable, even the roof was full; there was no lodging to be found anywhere. My father and his brother were in the square that night and, by chance, they came across a man and his young wife who had traveled a hundred and thirty kilometers from Nazareth. She was heavy with child and her time was almost due. My uncle was a shepherd, and they took pity on the young couple. I know that they brought them some fresh straw and a clay lamp with oil, and made a place for them up there in the cave."

"You said that you felt there was something different about the child. What did you mean by that?" Eric asked eagerly.

"I don't know exactly how to explain it. I remember my father talking to several groups of shepherds who said they had come in from the hills just to see the child. They all seemed very excited about something. I never really did know what all the commotion was about, but for several days I carried meals and water to them, and once the mother held the baby very near so I might see him clearly. I don't know; I can't explain it, but I just couldn't take my eyes off him. It was only a baby, but it was as if he held some sort of power over me." The man fell silent and just stood there with his memories of so many years ago.

"May I see the stable where this took place?" Eric asked, bringing him back to the present.

"You want to see the stable?" The man seemed surprised at the request.

"Please. It's very important to me," Eric pleaded.

"It's only a stable, like many others, but I will take you there if you like."

He took a lantern down from a hook on the wall and lit it from the lamp his wife was holding. He then opened the door and led Eric and Milcah down the narrow street leading out of the village.

Soon after they passed the last house, Silas left the dirt road and headed up a path on the hillside. The lantern offered only limited visibility and loose gravel slid from under their feet. A short distance further they came upon some openings in the rocks. The faint light revealed the outlines of sheep milling in the caves. Frightened by the intruders, they scampered out of the way. Inside one of the openings Silas held the lantern high and said," Here, this is where the child was born. It was as if he were in a dream; he couldn't believe he was actually standing there looking at it, this ordinary cave, where for years shepherds sheltered their sheep and goats, with no idea of the importance the world would one day place upon the site.

"It's everything... and it's nothing!" he finally muttered, not even knowing why he said it.

"I beg your pardon," the leather smith said. His arm was growing weary from the weight of the lantern.

"It was nothing," Eric replied. "We thank you very much for your hospitality, and for showing us this place."

"I hope you didn't think me a fool when I spoke of the child in such a manner. I was only a boy, but it has stayed with me all these years."

"I think nothing of the kind. I envy your experience," Eric assured him. "But we really must be on our way now. The hour grows late."

"Do you also think the child was special?" he asked Eric.

"There was an old man in Bethlehem at the time of which you speak, named Simeon, a righteous man to whom it had been divinely revealed that he would not see death before he had seen the Messiah. I feel sure, although not by promise, that you have been equally blessed."

With that, Eric took Milcah's hand and the three of them headed back down the path and into town. They thanked Silas again and left him standing outside his door holding the lantern, pondering Eric's remark.

Back at the caravan, they arranged their blankets on the ground under Ben Yaier's wagon. Eric knew that sleep would not come easy that night. They lay side by side, whispering to each other as Eric told Milcah more about the biblical account of the birth of Jesus. Eventually, though, they had to force themselves to try to sleep for tomorrow promised to be even more exciting - tomorrow they would be in Jerusalem!

CHAPTER XIII

Dawn broke to find Eric and Milcah still sound asleep. Normally, they were among the first to stir in the caravan but the events of the past night had allowed them only a few hours sleep. After a quick trip to the well to wash sleep from their eyes, their enthusiasm was restored and the excitement between them was contagious as they began the journey into Jerusalem, which would take less than two hours.

Ben Yaier soon joined them for some morning exercise. His manner was light, but Eric sensed that he had something on his mind. It didn't take long before he found out what.

"Eric," he began thoughtfully, "I've given considerable thought to what I'm about to say, so you please give some thought to it before answering."

"There's very little that you've ever said, my friend, that I don't give considerable thought to," Eric replied.

"What I have to propose may at first seem sometime risky and perhaps even a bit ludicrous, but I believe the benefits to be gained would outweigh the risks."

"Well, whatever you're laying the groundwork for you certainly did it in a way that has my attention. What is it you have in mind?"

"I'm going to suggest that when we reach Jerusalem you and Milcah stay with me for a while at the palace."

"At the palace?" Eric blurted out in surprise.

"Think for a moment, Eric, and I believe you'll follow my reasoning. If your young benefactor in Hebron keeps his word, the soldiers he 'detained' will be released soon, and the search for you two will be more intense than ever. You're going to need a place to hide, at least until the army finds something else to devote its priorities to."

"Yes, but the palace? Surely, of all places, it is crawling with soldiers."

"Think, man, do wolves hunt for prey in their own lair?"

The wisdom of Ben Yaier's remark caused Eric to pause to ponder what, at first, had seemed to be an insane idea.

"But how could you possibly hide us away?"

"I wouldn't."

"I don't understand," Eric said, with a puzzled expression.

"I wouldn't hide you away." He paused. "Do you recall Captain what's his name, who was about to arrest you back near Edh Dhahriye?"

"I won't soon forget that incident!"

"Well, I'm certain that news of that encounter has already reached Favious and probably Herod, too, so it should come as no great surprise when I arrive at the palace with a newly acquired servant and his wife. In fact, it may raise a question if I don't."

"After all you've done for us I would do anything in my power to spare you an embarrassing situation," Eric said with sincerity.

"Please my friend, do not base your decision on a concern for my safety. Should a question ever arise as to your whereabouts, I could always say that I sold you, or you ran away, and I would never be questioned further."

"But I just can't allow you to keep taking such risks for us," Eric said, although now he was being thoroughly swept away be the idea of having access to the palace itself.

"Allow an old man the excitement that can only come from taking risks. After all, to have seen with my own eyes, through those images you call photographs, the world of 2,000 years from now I would have risked or even given up my very life. So you see, Eric, I am more than compensated, and it is I who remain in your debt."

"I must admit," Eric's voice took on a ring of enthusiasm, "that the opportunity to see the inside of this building as it was, at a time when things happened which changed the world more than any other occurrence before or after, is probably more of a temptation than any scientist could resist."

"Then it is settled?"

"Only if you're sure it won't place you in any danger."

"I believe I would be in more danger with the two of you out there rambling around the desert looking for this man Jesus."

"I suppose you're right," Eric said in agreement.

"It's ridiculous for a man of science to 'suppose' about something that is so obviously logical. I'll ask again, is it settled?" "Yes, yes. Accepted with a gratitude we could never hope to repay."

"I thought we agreed earlier that indebtedness was merely a point of view, or perhaps your scholar Einstein would refer to it as relative."

"Ben Yaier, don't you feel it would be best if Eric remained in the role in which you originally cast him with Captain Fellini?" Milcah entered the conversation for the first time.

"What's that, my child?" A question designed to buy time while he attempted to sort out what she was talking about. Although he was thoroughly enchanted with Milcah, it was simply unheard of for a woman to offer an opinion or a suggestion. But then, he had also known, two minutes after Eric threw her into his wagon that this was no ordinary woman!

"I mean, that if Eric assumes the role of a foreigner of limited vocabulary would he not stand less chance of being engaged in conversation?"

"She's absolutely right, Eric. And not only that, but she remembered the name of the good Captain whose praises I must sing to Flavius. This will also give me an opportunity to learn just how much importance they place upon your capture."

"I quite agree," Eric said. "This business of being a fugitive was something that I really hadn't counted on. I'll welcome the opportunity of a cooling off place where we can gather news and plan the rest of our journey. And perhaps, as you said, the army will find something better to do with its time."

The rest of the journey was spent planning the roles they would play, while Eric and Milcah learned as much as they could about life and customs inside the palace.

Time passed quickly, and soon the great walls of the ancient city were in sight. Ben Yaier once again resumed his role as tour guide. Since the road from Bethlehem approached the city at an angle it would normally take the caravan to the gate at the northwest corner. Ben Yaier pointed out that the palace lay directly behind this wall to the south.

Yasmine told them that he had learned that the caravan would not be entering through this gate, but must make its way around the northern end of the city and enter through the Jericho gate. Eric and Milcah were delighted with the news; it was still early and this would give them an opportunity to see more of this magnificent city.

A quarter mile after the caravan turned north they came to a short road that cut off to the right, leading to another gate that was closed and unattended. Just to the left of the road was a small hill, not much bigger than a mound, that lay to their right between the main road and the city walls. Ben Yaier explained with reserved disgust that this was where the Romans executed condemned prisoners since Caesar had withdrawn the authority to do so from the Sanhedrin.

"Does this place have a name?" Eric asked.

"It is called Golgotha, the hill of Calvary."

Eric stopped abruptly and stared at the barren hill. A shout from the driver of the cart behind them jarred him back to reality, and they resumed walking. Still, Eric could not take his eyes off the hill.

"Is anything wrong?" Ben Yaier asked.

"Nothing," Eric shook his head.

As they rounded the northern wall in front of the gate where the road comes in from Galilee, Eric glanced back over his shoulder for one final look at the infamous hill that would mark the place where the ransom was paid and the end of Jesus' journey here on earth.

The northern wall formed a half circle that went on for over a kilometer before they reached the gate where the road came in from Jericho. The four towers of the fortress of Antonia loomed high above the walls themselves. This huge compound was adjacent to the northern wall of the temple area. The outer wall of the temple that enclosed the massive court of the Gentiles protruded out at least another three hundred yards in the direction of a hill beyond the Kidron Valley, overlooking the city. Ben Yaier told them that the hill was called the Mount of Olives.

Cobblestone replaced the dirt roads in front of all the gates. The heavy wheels of the carts and the oxen's hooves took on a rumbling sound as they rolled over the stones.

If Eric's memory served him right this gate would someday be known as the Gate of Saint Stephen, in memory of the first Christian martyr who was stoned to death here - a death that was to be witnessed by Paul before his conversion.

He had seen modern pictures of the walls and gates of the old city, but even allowing for the fact that the cobblestones they were walking on were paved in the pictures, and there were other signs of modern civilization, there was still something else different that he couldn't account for. He asked Ben Yaier if it would be any problem for the wagon to pull out of the caravan before entering the city, explaining that there was something he wanted to examine for a few moments. Ben Yaier told Yasmine to pull the wagon over to the side, allowing the others to pass.

Eric stood staring at the high gate, which had a somewhat pointed arch, perhaps thirty feet high and about fifteen feet wide. Inside a slight recess the actual entrance narrowed by a few feet and the height was reduced to about eighteen feet, with a less pronounced arch. Still, it did not look out of proportion set in the massive stone wall that rose over fifty feet. A small, flat decorative stone was directly over the gate, and above that was a more dominating structure about eight feet wide and ten feet high. It protruded out from the wall, supported by four stone braces. On both sides of it were what looked like windows that had outlived their usefulness and been sealed over with stone.

Several minutes passed while he continued to stare at the wall as if he expected it to change or something. Finally, Ben Yaier's curiosity got to him. "You're not some sort of modern day Joshua who intends to bring down our walls, are you?" he said, feeling somewhat guilty about breaking Eric's concentration.

"No, no," Eric replied with a smile. "It's just that something is out of place and I can't figure out what it is."

Ben Yaier looked at him with a puzzled expression. "How could something look out of place to a person who has never been here before?"

"I've seen photographs of this gate taken in the 20th century, and the wall looks exactly as it did in the photographs except..."

"Except what?" Ben Yaier asked with growing interest.

"I don't know," Eric said quietly, his gaze still fixed on the wall.

"Is it of any importance?" Ben Yaier asked.

"I guess not, since I can't even remember what it is I'm looking for."

"Would you like to continue on to the city, then?"

"Yes, by all means. You have no idea how anxious I am to see your city," Eric replied.

"If you're anywhere near as anxious to see the city as I am to take a hot bath, I think we should all be on our way."

"After you, Master," Eric made a bowing gesture.

"I'll thank you to say that with a little more conviction once we're in the palace," he said, smiling at Eric.

Eric returned the smile and they headed for the gate. Yasmine prodded the oxen into action.

The Roman guards had already been informed of Ben Yaier's expected arrival. As the wagon ground to a halt, the guards gave a courtesy salute to Ben Yaier, who was walking with Eric and Milcah, and motioned for them to pass through the gate.

Right at that inopportune moment Eric startled everyone within earshot by snapping his fingers and shouting in English, "I've got it!"

Immediately realizing what he had done, he whispered to Ben Yaier, "Could we possibly go back for a moment? I want to show you something."

The guard stepped forward and addressed Ben Yaier, but kept his gaze fixed on Eric.

"What did he say?"

"Nothing. Nothing at all. He has just a slight mental disorder that sometimes lends itself to bursts of enthusiasm in his native tongue. We will walk back for a spell before entering to allow his excitement to subside."

With that, Eric and Ben Yaier started walking back to the place where they had stood before, while Milcah stayed with Yasmine at the wagon. The guards only watched, one shrugging to the other in a gesture that implied "Don't ask me."

"By the way, what did you say back there?" Ben Yaier asked him. "And what's all the excitement about?"

"In spite of your talent for quick-witted fabrications to save my hide, in this you happened to have told that guard the truth...with the possible exception of the part about a mental disorder."

"Forgive me," Ben Yaier said with a faint smile, "it seemed appropriate at the time."

"I blurted out something in my native language without thinking. Should I ever do anything that stupid again, any reference to my mental disorder will remain undisputed."

"What is it you expect to see out here that you didn't see before?"

With that, Eric turned to look back at the wall. "There are no lions!"

Ben Yaier stared at him, bewildered. "Lion's?" he asked. "You expected there to be lions at the gates?"

"No, no, not real lions. Stone lions."

"Eric, what on earth are you talking about?"

"Forgive me, my friend, but this is something that hasn't happened yet. You see I studied as much as I could about your history before making my journey, and in the photographs I have seen of this gate. There are four carved stone lions, two on each side of the gate. They were ordered carved there by the Sultan Bibars, who stopped a horde of invading Mongols in the year 1260. By your calendar, that will not happen for about another 1230 years."

"Amazing," Ben Yaier whispered. "I don't suppose I'll ever get used to the idea that someone refers to future events as history."

"This is exactly the kind of proof I was looking for!" Excitement rang in Eric's voice.

"Proof of what?" Ben Yaier asked.

"Don't you see? If you take a photograph of me standing in front of this gate as it is today, without the carved lions, it will document the fact that the photograph was taken at least prior to the twelfth century."

"I still don't understand. Is there some doubt in your mind that your fellow scientists will believe you?" Ben Yaier asked.

"I've taken several photographs since I arrived, but nothing that couldn't be disputed or duplicated on a movie set."

"On a what?"

"I'll explain that later," Eric said as he dug in his pack for his camera and handed it to the old man who nearly dropped it, as the twelve ounce camera now weighed almost twenty five pounds.

"Sorry, I forgot," Eric said. "Can you hold it?"

"I'll manage," Ben Yaier assured.

"Just look through this little window until you see me, then make sure the gate and the wall, all the way to the top, are there. Whatever you see in there will be in the picture. Then just press the little button."

"Amazing," he repeated what had quickly become his most often used word.

"Will the guards question what we are doing?" Eric asked.

"No. Besides, their attention is much more appropriately focused on Milcah at the moment."

Eric posed, and Ben Yaier took the picture, handing the finished print to Eric as if he had just taken part in a miracle.

Looking at the photo, Eric uttered only one word, "Beautiful!"

"You or the lions?" Ben Yaier smiled.

"Me, of course," Eric countered.

As they walked back to the gate where they had left the wagon Ben Yaier's mood suddenly grew solemn. "When do you intend to return to the place from which you came?"

The question caught Eric off guard. It occurred to him how little thought he had given to the question, especially now that he was a fugitive.

"I don't know," Eric said. "I suppose I probably won't even think much about that until after I've found the man I came to see."

"You mean the one you call Jesus?"

"Yes," Eric nodded.

"I shall miss you but I will understand, because I, too, am a man of science. But I shall be concerned for Milcah."

Eric looked at him.

Ben Yaier looked back into his eye, but said nothing. There wasn't anything that needed to be put into words.

By the time they reached the wagon, Eric's mood had also grown solemn.

The guards merely acknowledged their return, but said nothing.

Ben Yaier signaled Yasmine, and they all proceeded into the city. Milcah's bright smile greeted them and almost immediately everyone*s mood was brightened by her contagious excitement as she relished her first visit to the holy city. Eric, too, was like a child at Disneyland as he strolled through the gates of history.

They entered through the lower part of the city, where the poorer people lived. The streets were narrow and the houses stacked tightly together. Shooting off in all directions were a maze of narrow passageways with stone stairways that made their way up hills where no cart could travel.

It wasn't long before they came to a broad intersection where, to the left, they could see wide steps that seemed unclimbable, leading up to the twin archways of the magnificent Antonia. Herod the Great had named his fortress palace in honor of his benefactor, Marc Antony. It was here, most historians believe, that Pilate held trial for Jesus.

Continuing south they came within sight of the great viaduct that cut across the entire city, linking Herod's palace with the temple and the Antonia. One could only marvel at the construction techniques, which allowed the builders to lift the huge limestone blocks into place using nothing more than colossal wooden cranes and manpower. Some of the blocks were more than thirty feet in length and cut so perfectly that they required no mortar.

After passing under one of the great arches of the viaduct they could catch an occasional glimpse of the wall that sectioned off the higher part of the city. Here, in their magnificent homes, the wealthy and influential lived in splendor. The architecture, showed both Greek and Roman influences, boasting pools and gardens of unequaled beauty, according to Ben Yaier's description.

They stopped as their road entered another wide intersection. From this vantage point they could see the steps leading to the southwest entrance of the temple. About fifteen degrees to the right of that could be seen the long, rectangular shape of the sports hippodrome stretching below the wall of the upper city. Off to the right, dominating the skyline was the upper part of the half-round theater, which was the cultural pride of Jerusalem.

Making their way west across the Tyropean Valley, their narrow road finally burst into the spacious open market in front of the palace. A U-shaped building in the center housed merchants of every sort. Here they catered only to the residents of the upper city and the palace itself, supplying the most exotic foods, expensive perfumes, garments, silverwork, jewelry, and luxuries of every kind.

Yasmine and the drivers continued on with the wagons, as Ben Yaier led his party towards the main entrance. He stopped at the bottom of the stairs and, with a smile on his kind face that magnified the lines at the corner of his eyes he announced, simply, "Welcome to Jerusalem."

As they climbed the steps, the huge planked doors seemed awesome, with thick horizontal metal bars that hung on equally massive hinges. Four uniformed palace guards who Ben Yaier explained were not Romans, stood watch. They recognized Ben Yaier as they approached and immediately gave him a tribute salute and signaled for the gates to be opened. Eric got a comfortable feeling from being under the protective wing of the highly respected Ben Yaier.

Inside the gates was a large courtyard. Within seconds after they entered, six men suddenly appeared out of one of the doors next to the steps that led up to the main entrance. Eric soon concluded that they were slaves, as they hurried to relieve Yasmine of his duties and began attending to the oxen and unloading the wagon that had entered the gate at ground level.

An older man who walked with a slight limp was obviously in charge of the group. He welcomed Ben Yaier back, and told him that the king was looking forward to an audience with him as soon as he had refreshed himself and felt up to it.

Calling him "Isaac," Ben Yaier thanked him and told him that he would attend the king shortly. Then he asked Isaac to have guest quarters prepared for Eric and Milcah.

One of the slaves attempted to relieve Eric of his pack. Eric thanked him politely, but said that he preferred to keep it with him.

Yasmine took over the supervisory duties as Isaac accompanied Ben Yaier, Milcah and Eric to their quarters.

They entered one of the doors leading from the courtyard and went through a short passageway that opened onto another courtyard that was a stunning contrast to the cold, indistinctive stone outer entrance. Here the grounds were pleasantly decorated with small trees and shrubs, complementing two large, round pools at each end. For the first time since his arrival, Eric saw flowers in bloom.

They ascended a stairway to an upper balcony that was supported by stone columns that arose from three sides of the garden. They arrived at Ben Yaier's door first, where he bade them farewell and made arrangements to see them later that day. Isaac wanted to see him settled in, but Ben Yaier insisted that he tend to Eric and Milcah instead.

They followed Isaac around the corner and down the full length of the balcony where he stopped and opened the door at the far end.

The room inside was spacious compared to those Eric had seen in Milcah's family home, but not as pretentious as one might expect to accommodate visiting dignitaries in a palace.

There was a long purple curtain hanging from an iron rod anchored to the ceiling that served as a partition separating the sleeping quarters from the main room. A glance at each other signaled their mutual relief at the fact that they could have some privacy as they carried out their facade of being husband and wife. However, Eric viewed the two beds occupying the area behind the curtain with mixed emotions.

Isaac asked whether they would like a tub sent to their chamber, or if they would rather bathe in the bathhouse pool. Eric requested a tub for Milcah, but said that he would prefer the pool.

As he was leaving, Isaac informed them that a woman would return shortly with cheese, fruit and wine.

When he closed the door, Eric and Milcah looked at each other for a moment, then Milcah jumped into his arms. He twirled her around and they shared in joyous laughter the good fortune that had befallen them. It was beyond their wildest dreams to have ended up not just safe, but protected in the king's own palace.

CHAPTER XIV

Ben Yaier approached the frail, balding man sitting behind a large table, surrounded by two muscular guards who made him seem even smaller than he was. Painfully near-sighted, his large nose nearly touched the record ledger that he was writing in when Ben Yaier greeted him.

"Good day, Riphath."

He looked up at Ben Yaier through squinted eyes, which desperately attempted to focus on the face from which the greeting had come.

"Ah, Ben Yaier, the king has been expecting you. He gave me orders to admit you the moment you arrive." He spoke in a matter-of-fact monotone voice, perfected over years of refusing an audience to those holding no interest to the king.

Even before Riphath's signal, the two guards opened the door leading to the king's chamber.

Herod was alone in the massive throne room, a condition seldom seen by Ben Yaier. As the door opened, he rose from behind the ornately carved marble table where he was seated. He was a homely man, whose individual features did nothing to compliment his round face which, in lieu of a neck was coupled directly to a pathetically unconditioned body by a bloated double chin. Although not yet forty, years of pampered living, a lack of enthusiasm for any type of physical exercise, and an appetite for indulgence all contributed to the dissipated specimen walking toward Ben Yaier with outstretched arms.

"God, how I've missed you!" Herod said in a deep baritone that was ridiculously mismatched to his physical appearance. He embraced Ben Yaier.

"Even as I have missed being in the presence of my King," he responded.

Ben Yaier detested politics, but found himself too closely enmeshed in the inner workings of the court to avoid them completely. It was for this reason that he had diplomatically bestowed the unauthorized title of king upon Herod. Born Antipas, he was the son of Herod the Great, the hated ruler of this remote eastern outpost of Rome's Mediterranean empire, and the last Jewish ruler to bear the title of king.

At his death, Herod's will divided the territory into three areas. Antipas was to share power with his older brother Archelaus, his half brother Phillip, and his father's sister, Salome. This transfer could not take place, however, until the Emperor Augustus ratified the will. When the power struggle began within the family, the fragmented kingdom was in rebellious turmoil. All three brothers eventually traveled to Rome to gain the favor of the procrastinating Augustus, who eventually gave the title of Ethnarch upon Archelaus, withholding the title of king until he proved himself worthy. Antipas and Phillip were given the lesser title of Tetrarch. However, Archelaus' oppressiveness, in which he followed his father, soon caused his downfall and banishment to Gaul.

When Antipas came to power he took the name of Herod and brought relative peace to Judah until Pontius Pilate arrived as governor. Although never granted the title of king, those close to him, desiring to remain in favor, addressed him as such within the palace.

"As your king, I order you never to go away again for such a long period of time," Herod said, grasping Ben Yaier's shoulders.

"You flatter me, Your Majesty."

"You wouldn't think it flattery if it had been me leaving you surrounded by a tribe of insensitive baboons to counsel with."

"Oh come now," Ben Yaier said. "I have never given you any assistance with the affairs of state."

"Rome has seen to it that the affairs of state require little more than warm buttocks to heat the cold seat of the throne.

No, my friend, the emptiness of which I speak grew out of my need to share more personal matters."

"If there is anything troubling your Majesty at the moment, then I am pleased that my ears are now in Jerusalem."

"I only wish that you could have been with me when it happened. I wanted desperately to confer with you on a decision that was forced upon me."

"Would it serve any purpose to speak of it now?"

"It wasn't my fault," Herod began, his mood solemn. "There is so much unrest in the land. Pilate continues with his inexhaustible list of items subject to new taxes. The High Priest clamors at me to take stronger action against the fanatics who pose a threat to our God, and to their power, with all this talk of messiahs. There was one, in particular, whom I swear had a personal vendetta against me. The fool would come regularly outside the palace and condemn me for my marriage to Herodias because she was Phillip's wife. Neither, the High Priest Caiaphas, nor his father-in-law Annas, who judged even more critically when he held the office, made such a condemnation. But this madman took it upon himself to engage in a public confrontation with his King."

"Was it not possible to simply forbid him from speaking out against you in public?"

"There was no reasoning with this radical. He was somehow associated with that other trouble maker who is still stirring things up around Galilee."

"Was?" Ben Yaier asked.

"It wasn't my fault," Herod said, his voice rising defensively. "I fell into a trap that could only have been conceived in the mind of a woman with the cunning of Herodias. To still his voice, I had ordered the arrest of this one they call the Baptist, who had been persecuting me, and had him interned at Machaerus." He paused before continuing. "Ever since her daughter, Salome, first blossomed, each time my eyes fell upon her, she would set my soul on fire... it was the night of my birthday feast and the wine had gone to my head.

She was reclining next to her mother and my passion kept growing in me as I pleaded with her to dance for the guests. At last the girl consented. As I watched her I became so inflamed with the need to possess her that I granted her any wish she named, up to half my kingdom. She could have had gold, jewels, slaves, anything she wanted, but her mother influenced her to ask for the head of the Baptist. That was when I needed you more than I ever had before! What was I to do? Can a king go back on his word that he has given before witnesses? Yes, I kept my word and granted her request...and the ghost of that man has haunted me ever since." "Perhaps you have concerned yourself too much with the matter." Ben Yaier began, his words sounding inadequate to him as he sensed the depths of the king's despair. "As for myself I can only feel grateful that such decisions are never forced on me, but for kings and generals decisions of this nature are an unfortunate part of their destiny. They do what they must, then bear in loneliness the results of those deeds, as no ordinary man could understand."

"You do understand, my old tutor, but only partially. Keep in mind that the blood of my father flows in these veins, the same blood that ordered the execution of his favorite wife, Mariamne, and her mother. Even three of his own sons he had put to death, to say nothing of the priests and scribes whom he suspected of being in opposition to him. It is a rich heritage, indeed, this blood that my father passed on to me. Even his slaughter of all the infants in Bethlehem failed to unnerve him. As for me, I have no stomach for such a thing. But nevertheless, on more than one occasion I have had men put to death in secret and reveled in drunken orgies that very same night...but, this man was different. I can't explain it, but there was something about him...something I have never felt before. My blood now runs cold with fear. I awake at night in a cold sweat from dreams where I see his head being carried in to me on a platter....his head becomes my own."

Herod fell silent, staring straight ahead, his back to Ben Yaier.

Feeling helpless, Ben Yaier said the only thing he could think of, "Perhaps a change of scene would be of some benefit."

"We journeyed to Masada, returning only eight days ago. It was a miserable trip, and I rushed back hoping that you would have returned from Egypt," he said, his mood lightening slightly.

"It grieves me that I wasn't available for whatever assistance I might have been able to give you, your Majesty, but the caravan was pitifully slow."

"And how was your trip?" Herod asked, determined to shift the subject away from what was so painful to him. "I received word about you from somewhere near Hebron. Something about a person with you being mistaken for a fugitive."

"Oh, that," Ben Yaier smiled and stalled. He really hadn't planned to bring up the subject of Eric and Milcah at this time. "I met this couple in the caravan and we became quite close. The man has a profound knowledge of a mathematics that is revolutionarily different than our system, and he agreed to teach me. He has only a limited knowledge of our tongue, but then, mathematics is a language all its own so we communicate quite adequately. I took the liberty of asking them to be guests here in the palace for a while until we finish our studies. I hope this meets with your approval."

"Whoever you would invite would be welcome here, my old friend. I'm just glad you've finally returned. In fact, in honor of your return we shall have a banquet tonight." Herod's mood had become festive. "Yes, yes, it's been too long since there has been any joy in this dismal place," he said, putting his arm around Ben Yaier's shoulder. "Tonight we shall celebrate your return, but for now you must rest."

"Isn't that rather short notice to prepare such an under-taking, even for Herod?"

"Let me revel in the joy of your homecoming. It's been far too long since this weary soul of mine has felt the urge to celebrate. I have no wish to deny myself that pleasure for another day."

"I'm rather weary from the journey," Ben Yaier said, as he prepared to leave.

"Of course," Herod replied. "Tell Ripath to summon Ophelia and I'll make arrangements for the feast and invitations."

As Ben Yaier was going out the door, Herod shouted, "Be sure to invite your guests. I want to meet the man who knows something you don't know," he laughed.

Ben Yaier went up to Eric and Milcah's chamber and recounted the things Herod had said.

Eric's mind was spinning from the things Ben Yaier told him. If John had already been slain then the time when Jesus would make his journey into Jerusalem could not be far off. He still couldn't believe that he had arrived so close to the most significant event in the history of mankind and yet no one was aware of it.

Eric's voice was barely audible, but very intense, as he asked Ben Yaier, "When do you begin the celebration of Passover?"

"In nine days. Why do you ask?"

"Oh my God!" Eric whispered.

"What is it, Eric?" Milcah asked, at a loss to understand his reaction.

"Jesus is probably in Jerusalem now."

"Oh, Eric, how wonderful!" Milcah was excited.

"Then you'll be able to see him," Ben Yaier said. "But how do you know his whereabouts?"

"The time is so close," Eric whispered.

"What time is so close, Eric?" Milcah was puzzled. "Why aren't you happy? I thought this is what you wanted."

"Forgive me," he asked of both of them. "I just didn't expect it to be like this...I mean at this time!"

Ben Yaier and Milcah looked at each other with expressions of bewilderment.

"I'm sorry, my friend, but we were under the impression that you made your incredible journey to seek out this man. "Now, somehow, you react with sadness. Can you help us to understand this?" Ben Yaier asked in a kind voice.

"I'm sorry," Eric said. "Do you recall when I mentioned that this man's followers would write of his life and works?"

They both nodded without speaking.

"Well, they also wrote of his death and the events leading up to it, even though they themselves never fully understood why. It is from then - writings that I know where Jesus is now - and that his time on earth is very short."

They both sat in silence.

"What will happen to him?" Milcah finally spoke.

"He will be crucified,"

"Oh, God, no!" Milcah put her hand over her mouth.

"Why?" Ben Yaier blurted out. "Who will do this, and why?"

"The priests see him as a threat to their power. Herod will see him as a threat to his throne as he speaks of a kingdom that he cannot understand. Pilate will see him as a troublemaker whose silence would relieve him of the pressures brought on by this conflict, so it will be Rome that will nail him to the stake."

"Eric, I have only heard fleeting tales of this man, and I don't know what crimes He will be accused of, but perhaps if I spoke to Herod he might reconsider and possibly influence Pilate."

"Herod is but an instrument, playing his role in history."

"But you, then," Milcah pleaded, "surely you have the means in that un-budge-able bag of yours to stop a whole Roman Legion if you choose to."

"You don't understand, Milcah. Jesus has the power to move mountains, but He will choose to die."

"But why," she persisted, "why, if he has the power to prevent it would he choose to die."

"But why," she persisted," why, if He has the power to prevent it would be choose to die?"

"Actually, it is not His choice, but that of God, His father in heaven. Jesus will simply obey His will."

"But how is it possible for a father who loves his son to want to see him suffer so?" She was sobbing now.

160

"For millenniums, your priests have been shedding the blood of sacrificial lambs on their altars, according to law, for the atonement of sins, but only the finest lamb in the flock was acceptable. The one you call Jehovah has offered His Son's blood as atonement for all the people of the world in order to redeem mankind from the sins they inherited from Adam and Eve."

"But..." Milcah started...

"But hell!" Eric shouted in English, suddenly angry with frustration. "Don't ask me why this is, or why that! I know the answers the scrolls give, but that doesn't mean I have all the whys. Whys are what I came here for. Had it been me dealing with old Lucifer when he caused all that trouble in Eden, I'd have just said, 'Hey, I'm the boss here. We don't have room for troublemakers' and squashed him right there, putting an end to it." His angry voice subsided. "I could never understand why it was necessary for the whole world to suffer for the sins of two people."

"Does the death of this man change the world?" Ben Yaier asked.

"His teachings will have a great impact, but we still have poverty, hatred, hunger, wars, greed, and, in my time, we have a world so divided by political turmoil that all nations live in constant fear of total annihilation."

"Was his death, then, meaningless?" Ben Yaier asked.

Eric's eyes met his. "I don't know. I only know that I must speak to him before it is too late."

"Do you know exactly where to find him?"

"No, but it is recorded that at this time he was preaching in the temple during the day but his party was encamped at a place called the Mount of Olives. Good Lord!" Eric nearly exploded. "Do you think he might be there now?"

"I have no way of knowing, but now is not the time to find out. The palace tailor will be here soon to fit both of you for suitable garments to wear to the king's banquet tonight."

"The king's banquet?" Eric turned in surprise. "Why would we attend the king's banquet?"

"Because he has invited you."

"But why?"

"Kings are not obliged to give reasons."

"Well, it's just too dangerous. We'll be found out. We'll have to find a way to decline his invitation."

"An invitation from some may be considered a request, but an invitation from a king does not leave one any option."

Eric thought for a moment. "Of course. I wasn't thinking very clearly. It's just that knowing that Jesus might be just over there..."

There was a knock at the door. It was the tailor, attended by four women bearing bolts of fabric and the tools of his trade.

Ben Yaier left them to their fitting. Eric and Milcah responded like robots to the tailor's instructions and questions as they pondered this new development.

Eric wanted to dash from the room and run to the temple, and only the knowledge of the embarrassment and danger it would cause Ben Yaier and Milcah, kept him from doing so. He could never have imagined such an absurd set of circumstances that could make an appointment with a tailor take precedence over the opportunity to possibly see Jesus.

The tailor's assistants were still gathering up the last of their patterns and fabrics when two men came in carrying a heavy bronze tub, followed by six women bearing water and perfumes for Milcah's bath. One of the women handed Eric a robe, towel and sandals for his use at the palace pools.

Damn this banquet, Eric thought. Nero fiddled while Rome burned. The Lord may be less than a mile away and I take a bath. Surely insanity could not be less rational!

One of the tub bearers accompanied him down two flights of stairs to the bath pools. The room was empty except for them. The large man, whom Eric guessed to be Ethiopian, did not speak but stationed himself a few feet away.

In the soothing hot mineral waters Eric's tension began to subside. It was the closest thing to a narcotic he had ever experienced. As his brain raced without direction from thoughts of Wendell Perry, to Saul, to Milcah, to Bethlehem, to all that had happened to him or was about to happen, everything began to blend into a whirling kaleidoscope of meaningless color. Each thought lost its particular significance as one blended into another: colors being stirred by some invisible brush on an artist's palette.

He did nothing to resist the whirlpool of serenity he felt himself drifting into; he didn't want to resist. Perhaps, he remembered thinking, a person's brain needs some sort of temporary rebellion against sanity to prevent insanity from taking over permanently. Deeper and deeper he drifted with the current as the warm waters enveloped his body. His mind reached a state of total, weightless contentment that soon gave way to a deep, restful sleep.

He only napped for about fifteen minutes, but when the attendant awakened him it was as if he had slept a full night. After an invigorating massage he returned to the room, where Milcah was being attended behind the curtain.

A new garment, completed only minutes ago, lay draped over a couch and a new pair of sandals was neatly tucked below. He wasted no time in slipping into them as the steady stream of chatter continued behind the curtain.

Feeling more relaxed than at any time he could remember he poured himself a goblet of wine, reclined on the couch, and was enjoying a fresh fig when the two women that had been attending to Milcah appeared from behind the curtain and hurried out the door.

A few seconds later, Milcah stepped out. Eric could say or do nothing. He had never seen a woman as beautiful as she. In a single, perhaps trite, but often inappropriately used word, she was breathtaking!

Finally she spoke, "You think I look foolish." It was a statement rather than a question.

He got up from the couch and came to her. Taking her hand in his, he said softly, "If you look foolish, then so do the desert flowers after a rain."

Ever so slowly they came together. Their lips touched softly then blended with fury as he drew her close to him.

Once again the fires of passion ignited them, only this time it was Eric who gently retreated from the embrace.

"I want you at this moment more than I've ever wanted anything in my life. Lamentably, this sometimes painfully logical brain of mine has given me at least a dozen reasons why I should stop listening to my pounding heart and respect the things we both believe in."

"I know very well that someday my pounding heart will thank your logical brain," she smiled and sighed, "but please don't ask it of me right now."

He kissed her gently on the forehead.

"Do you intend to offer me some wine?" she said playfully. "I've never attended a king's banquet before, and I believe I'm going to need all the courage the grapes can provide."

"Allow me to pour for you, m'lady, and perhaps we can dazzle the royalty together with our sophisticated hiccups."

An hour later Ben Yaier came to their room to accompany them to the banquet. He complimented them on their appearance and was so delighted with the gay mood the wine had provided his apprehensive friends that he joined them in another goblet before they started their journey through the palace to the banquet hall.

As they entered the huge hall Eric couldn't help but think of what a remarkable job modern movie-makers had done in reproducing scenes like the one before him. There was an outer and inner circle of columns supporting the roof, and the smell of oil torches filled the air. Reclining couches were everywhere, many already occupied by early arrivals. Musicians accompanied two dancers in the center of the room, where the king's couch was slightly elevated above the rest. Herod, by protocol, had not yet arrived.

Several of the guests greeted Ben Yaier as they made their way through the crowd to their place of honor, next to the king.

Each padded mat had a large pillow at its head and a small serving table by its side. Ben Yaier placed Milcah between himself and Eric. Within seconds, they were served wine and a small plate of appetizers, which included cakes, figs, jellyfish, and fungi.

The tempo of the music increased as the woman dancers whirled, ending abruptly face down on the floor in front of them.

Eric wondered if applause was in order, but saw that the crowd continued drinking and chattering as if the dancers didn't exist. The two women ran off, heads bowed, and were instantly replaced by three acrobats who started a series of tumbling and balancing routines. They drew even less attention than the dancers.

Eric started to say something to Milcah, but was interrupted by the arrival of two guests who occupied the places next to him. They, too, had obviously shared some fruit of the vine a bit earlier. Eric couldn't be sure if their loud voices were due to too much wine or merely a need to draw attention to them. They were dressed in expensive garments, and both wore excessive amounts of jewelry, with rings decorating all of their fingers. Their rotund stomachs indicated that they both also shared a taste for gluttony.

The fatter and drunker of the two eased himself onto the mat next to Eric and greeted him in a pompously polite manner that took care not to offend anyone whose status merited a position closer to the king than his.

"My name is Joktan, Judean Minister of Finance, and with whom do I have the pleasure of speaking?"

Eric knew that it was time to go into his act if he were to keep future conversation with his newly acquired dinner companion to a minimum. He struggled in very broken Aramaic, "My name Eric...Ben Yaier speak stay this place. Speak very bad your language. Sorry."

"Oh, I see, you're a friend of Ben Yaier's," he said coldly.

"Friend, yes friend," Eric said smiling, like one satisfied when he is able to understand a word in another language.

"And where are you from?" Joktan questioned further.

Eric looked at him blankly. "Sorry, no understand," he said.

"What language do you speak?"

Eric continued staring.

"Live...where do you live...what country?"

"Sorry."

"Do you speak Greek?"

"Ah, no Greek. Sorry."

Convinced that he would have to seek dinner conversation elsewhere, and confident that Eric would not understand, he sighed and said directly to him, "You are a rather sorry bastard at that."

Eric just smiled at him and repeated, "Yes, sorry."

Joktan turned away and resumed his conversation with his companion.

Safe in knowing the gesture would be meaningless even if someone should see it, Eric took the opportunity of flipping his hand toward Joktan in a sign that doesn't require the use of four of the finger's on one's hand.

Milcah was watching and of course asked, "What does that mean?"

Eric cringed and laughed, "My God, woman, does nothing escape you?"

"Tell me what it means," she said with a little giggle.

"Nothing," he smiled, "it doesn't mean anything."

"I'll bet it's something like the honorary title you bestowed upon my uncle, isn't it."

Eric laughed out loud remembering the laughing jag they had shared over that incident. "You're close enough. Now shut up and eat your grapes.

With that, a loud trumpet blare filled the hall. It didn't require any explanation for Eric to know that Herod was about to enter the hall.

The large curtains directly behind them parted, and Herod entered with Herodias on his arm. Everyone in the hall bowed in their direction as they walked to the place next to Ben Yaier.

Herod shouted, "Welcome to the feast in honor of the scholar, Ben Yaier," which seemed to be the signal for the festivities to resume.

He greeted Ben Yaier and said, "So these are the guests of whom you spoke so highly. But you failed to mention how lovely this one is," taking Milcah's hand.

"I'm afraid the desert dust and wind obscured things that even I did not see until today, your Majesty."

"I find it hard to believe that there is enough dust in all Judea to hide such beauty, you old fox. You enjoy holding back on me. And this must be the learned one," he said, reluctantly turning his attention to Eric.

"May I introduce your Majesty to Eric of Britannica, and his wife, Milcah, whose father resides in Beersheba." Then, speaking loud enough for Herodias to hear, "And her Majesty, the Queen."

Herodias nodded with little interest and turned her attention in the opposite direction, obviously annoyed at Herod's attention to Milcah.

"Come, let us drink to your return, my friend." With that, Herod emptied a full goblet of wine, which was just as quickly refilled by a young woman who knelt behind him.

Herod had a sobering effect on Eric as he watched him guzzling wine and wallowing in his own importance. Of all the rulers of all the nations the world has known, some good, some bad, most have been forgotten by history because their contribution (or, more precisely, their lack of same) has had such little effect upon changing or shaping the course of events. Here, he thought, was the perfect example of a man who, had it not been for birthrights, could not have ruled over a chicken coop. Yet, as he sits here tonight he has no way of knowing that his only claim to a place in history will be due to his brief encounter with a man he has yet to meet.

Two wrestling midgets had replaced the acrobats.

Eric's attention was caught when the boisterous pair next to him used the word "Baptist." They were now speaking softly enough to be sure Herod did not hear, but they felt secure in their knowledge that Eric couldn't understand them.

"I mean, I really didn't appreciate being given such short notice to prepare for this. At least for his birthday feast we were given a month's notice, even if we did have to travel halfway around the Dead Sea to Machaerus."

"This is the first banquet he's given since then."

"Well frankly, my friend, after having gorged myself on mutton, truffles and wine all night I must say it didn't have a very settling effect on my stomach, either."

"I'm not saying it was in the best of taste, Joktan, but I was watching Herod's face when the guard brought it in. I'm telling you, he turned white."

"I wonder what he'll do to top that tonight?"

"Maybe he'll go out and get that other one, the one who caused the trouble the other day."

"Who's that?"

"The one who caused all the ruckus at the court of the Gentiles, knocking things around and swinging a rope at everyone."

"Swinging a rope."

"That's what I heard. He claimed it was his father's house and he drove them all right out of there, swinging a rope at the moneychangers."

"That's the world coming to? Say what you will, Rome has made life pretty good for us. So why do all these radical, religious fools keep stirring things up? Do you have any idea what it does for the economy when Jews from Persia, Babylonia, Greece and everywhere else return to Jerusalem for the Passover? They have to change their foreign currency for shekels somewhere."

"I've heard that nearly every day he gets into some confrontation or other with the priests of the temple over who's right or wrong."

"Who does he think he is?"

"Some people were saying that he thinks he's the Son of God."

"Is he insane, or just a drunkard?"

"I don't know, but he draws large crowds wherever he goes and I'm told that a lot of people believe him. They're probably all Pharisees jealous of the position the Sadducees hold on the Sanhedrin."

"That's just the sort of thing that causes trouble. He should be stopped."

"Don't worry. He'll go too far one of these days and then Caiaphas will see to him."

"Where's that slut with the wine?"

It was all Eric could do to remain silent. He wanted desperately to jump up and yank them off their wine laden rumps and shout, "You fools, you poor, stupid fools! You don't know what you're saying."

Instead, he turned to Ben Yaier and said softly, "How improper would it be if we were to leave?"

"Is something wrong?"

"Everything is wrong, and I can't do anything about it."

"Has the wine given you a headache?"

"It's not the wine."

"I prefer not to shun the king. However, if you feel that you must leave..."

"No, no," Eric said. "I'm sorry, I'm acting impulsively." He felt thoughtless for not having considered the embarrassment their leaving would cause Ben Yaier.

"The food will be served shortly."

"I think what I need is some more wine, and I'll stick a grape in my right ear."

Ben Yaier looked at him with a curious smile. "I suppose that is another strange custom of the fifth millennium that you'll tell me about one day."

Eric leaned back on his own couch with Milcah, who had overheard the conversation, between them. She was just looking at Eric, not saying anything, but with that unmistakable look of wanting to ask a question.

Eric looked her straight in the eye and said, "No, we don't go around sticking grapes in our ears."

She put her hand over her mouth and snickered. She lightened Eric's mood, as only she could.

The food arrived, an elaborate main course of flamingo tongues, wild boar and lobster. They drank more wine, as a large, heavy man, who seemed hairier than his opponent, wrestled with a bear.

Both during and after dinner a great deal more wine was consumed. If there was a social code for behavior at such royal affairs, few of the guests seemed aware of it. There may have been a few wives present but, judging from the activity in the room, it seemed that most of the women were either provided by Herod or else were professional escorts who were never invited to attend family affairs.

Eric sensed that Milcah was beginning to feel uncomfortable, as some of the groups grew bolder in their drunken passion. No one seemed to pay any attention to the lustful frolicking that was beginning to take place, with the possible exception of one couple who, in a spontaneous lateral movement, sought to enhance their pleasure with another consenting couple.

He felt relieved, however, that two or three women alternated in keeping Herod occupied. His earlier attraction to Milcah could have developed into a problem in this licentious atmosphere. Eric smiled at the thought of the volumes of written protocol in various government libraries throughout the world. Where is there one written on the subject of how to tell a horny king to buzz off and find his own girl?

Eric was considering broaching the subject of their leaving again with Ben Yaier, who was involved in conversation with one of the few guests still not hopelessly intoxicated. Suddenly he felt Milcah's hand clutch his arm.

She said nothing at first, as Eric followed her concerned stare toward some men walking behind the first row of pillars at the hall, oblivious to the merry makers around them.

"Isn't that..." she didn't finish.

Eric squinted, as if to see more clearly. There were four palace guards, and a fifth man.

"Oh my God," Eric said in English. It was Saul.

CHAPTER XV

Eric had Milcah turn her head the other way to avoid being recognized. He held up his goblet so it covered most of his face but still let him monitor the direction the group took. He breathed a sigh of relief as they continued straight ahead and left the hall through a side entrance.

Nevertheless, as long as Saul was in the palace the danger was still there. That old devil of uncertainty reared its ugly head again. That's the one that assures you that no matter what you do, it will probably be wrong. Still, it screams with equal authority, Do Something! At that moment he only knew that he had to explain the situation to Ben Yaier and leave the banquet immediately.

After hearing him out, Ben Yaier agreed, but insisted upon accompanying them back to their quarters. He didn't want to risk their running into Saul unescorted. They would not be missed now that the festivities had degenerated to the point where most of the guests were preoccupied with one form of self-indulgence or other.

Ben Yaier said something to Herod, who simply smiled and waved him off, as he was far more interested in fondling the breast of the young girl pouring his wine.

They made their way through the sea of bodies and out into the hallway, and arrived at their room without incident.

"You'll be safe here," Ben Yaier tried to reassure them. "I'll return to the banquet and plant myself next to Favious. If there is any urgency regarding Saul's presence here he would be the first to be informed."

"Please let us know the instant you hear anything," Eric pleaded, "no matter when that might be."

"I promise." Ben Yaier tried to muster a smile as he reached for the door.

"Ben Yaier," Eric called after him.

"Yes?"

"I'm not sure what this night will hold, but tomorrow it is imperative that I go to the temple."

"I understand." His voice was filled more with empathy than permission.

After he closed the door, Eric and Milcah settled down into an uneasy wait, pondering what fate had in store for them.

Where did it get all screwed up, Eric thought to himself. Why did I ever allow Milcah to get involved? If only I hadn't flashed that damn light out onto the desert that first night maybe none of this would have happened. My God, is it possible that I could get this far, only to spend the rest of my life rotting in some Roman dungeon?

He had to reprimand himself for allowing negative thinking to fill his head. Right now his main priority had to be Milcah's safety. He didn't feel there was anything he could do until they heard from Ben Yaier, so he thought that while they waited he would do what he could to lighten the mood.

"I like the party here much better than the one back at the zoo." he said, trying his best to sound cheerful. "Would you care for some wine?"

"No, thank you." She forced a smile. "I think I've already had more than enough." She paused for a moment, and then gave him that inquiring look he had come to know so well. "Eric?"

"Yes, m'lady?"

"Is that what they call a banquet in your America?"

"What?"

"A zoo. It sounded like you said 'zoo.'"

He had pulled his old boo-boo of using an English word when he didn't know the Aramaic equivalent.

"Oh, no," he smiled. "That's just an expression. I mean a zoo is a place where they keep animals."

"Like a stable?"

"Well, not exactly."

"I see," she giggled a little. "You're comparing the behavior of the king's guests to animals."

"Come to think of it, that's not fair. Most animals I've seen have more dignity."

"Oh Eric, you're terrible! I'm going to stop asking you the meaning of your America words. Besides that, I've changed my mind. I will have some wine."

He smiled and poured. "O.K., no America words."

"O.K.?" She gave him an impish grin. "What does 'O.K.' mean?"

He just shook his head and smiled.

They drank wine and passed the time with light talk to make the waiting easier; hoping all the while that a knock on the door would be Ben Yaier and not the palace guards.

Finally the knock came.

They both jumped and gave each other a brief look that revealed their mutual apprehension. Eric moved to the door and lifted the latch.

It was Ben Yaier. A sigh of relief, then he welcomed him in.

"Were you able to learn anything?" Eric asked anxiously.

"Only that you may sleep well tonight. I stayed until Favious retired to his quarters with a companion. I know from past performances that he will be occupied well into tomorrow, and no one will dare disturb him."

"And no messages were brought to him?"

"None."

"Whew!" This time Eric made no attempt to hide the apprehension he had been feeling.

"Ben Yaier," Eric began hesitantly, "you've already done so much for us that I am very reluctant to ask you for another favor, but I don't know where else to turn."

"What is it, my friend?"

"This whole situation has gotten out of hand. Is there any way you can help me get Milcah back to her father's house?"

"No, Eric!" Milcah sprang from the couch. "No, please, no! It just isn't fair! We're so close. Perhaps tomorrow we'll be able to see him. Besides, I'm not leaving you."

"Milcah," he shouted and grabbed her shoulders. She grimaced with pain as he had temporarily forgotten his strength. "I'm sorry," he said softly. "It's just become too dangerous. We didn't count on any of this when I promised your father that I would take care of you."

"I don't care. I don't care about anything." Her protests grew more vehement as her voice began to shake. "You promised. We've come so far." She was searching for any argument she could use in her cause. "You said that your scrolls told you that he was soon to die. Oh please, Eric, don't deprive me of the chance to see him!"

Eric was looking deep into her eyes that were now beginning to well with tears. He was torn between doing what he thought was best for her safety and prolonging the risk in the hope of fulfilling a need she felt so strongly, a need that he understood all too well.

"Perhaps, Eric," Ben Yaier said softly, "Saul's presence here is only a coincidence and has nothing at all to do with you and Milcah."

"That's right," Milcah was quick to respond, grateful to Ben Yaier for a supporting argument that had escaped her. "Perhaps he just comes here all the time."

"Very well," Eric said, and before he could get another word out Milcah jumped in, grabbed a big hunk of his hair, and pulled his head down and kissed him.

Ben Yaier smiled his approval.

"God, woman, is there no end to your wanton indiscretions?"

"None," she bubbled.

"Why do I feel like the victim of a conspiracy?"

"Because we're two thousand years older than you. That ought to give us some negotiating advantage," she said smugly, squeezing Ben Yaier's hand.

"Well, it's obvious that I'm not in the same class with you two. But to get back to our immediate problem: It would be naive to think that Saul has forgotten the incident or wouldn't recognize either of us again should we meet, so we must leave the palace."

"Where will you go?" Ben Yaier asked.

"Tomorrow we wait at the temple. If Jesus does not come we have to leave the city and go to the Mount of Olives."

"That's the hill you saw this morning just behind the temple," Ben Yaier said. "Try to find a place where one might logically rendezvous, and if I need to get a message to you I will send Yasmine at dawn, noon, or sunset."

"Thank you, my friend." Eric put his hands on Ben Yaier's shoulders. "And what a friend you have been."

Ben Yaier reached into a small pouch hanging from his sash. "Here, take this," handing him a small gold medallion. "It will allow you passage through the palace and city gates. No one will question it."

Eric went to his pack and got out the collection of twentieth century photographs. "Here," he said, "I want you to have these."

The two men just stood there for a moment. Eric could see moisture welling up in the old man's eyes.

"I have this dreadful feeling that I won't be seeing you two again." Ben Yaier said, trying to summon up a smile.

"God willing, that won't be true," Eric said softly. "But where we go, you will always be with us."

The two men embraced each other. Ben Yaier held out one arm and Milcah joined them. Tears flowed freely down her cheeks as she kissed both of them and melted into the warmth of the embrace. They just stood there in silence swaying ever so gently to some nonexistent melody, sharing in the love being generated within that circle. None was willing to break it, for they all knew too well that this moment of magic could never be captured again...and yet would never be lost.

Ben Yaier whispered one final thing before he turned and left the room: "Go with God."

CHAPTER XVI

It was mid-morning when they arrived at the temple. It was truly a magnificent example of a simple architectural plan, with the central sanctuary surrounded by a series of spacious outer courts, each progressively more exclusive.

Eric and Milcah entered through one of a series of double arched gates into the massive outermost Court of the Gentiles, a huge area covering nearly thirty-five acres, paved with colored stones and enclosed by tall, stately columns. It was crowded with people from all walks of life. Many were merchants selling doves, young cattle, and sheep for sacrifice. Moneychangers were everywhere.

In the center stood an enclosed compound with signs posted on it warning that non-Jews were forbidden to enter under penalty of death. This led into an inner court known as the Court of Women. Eric decided not to enter even though Milcah could have done so safely, for the penalty for satisfying his curiosity seemed to far outweigh the possible reward. Besides, it was in the Court of Gentiles that Jesus was said to be doing his preaching.

They would stay here and try to remain inconspicuous, even though Eric would have given his eyeteeth to see the things he had only read about that lay beyond the Court of Women, in the Court of Priests. It was described as being built of perfectly tooled white marble covered with plates of heavy gold. Golden spikes soared to a height of 165 feet from the roof. At the back of a large porch there was said to be immense gilded doors covered with blue, crimson, purple and golden tapestry. Significant above this was a golden vine, symbolizing the nation of Israel.

It was agonizing to be so close to such a significant structure and not be able to see it. There was, however, only one priority worth risking everything for, and they must do nothing to jeopardize their chance of that happening.

They stationed themselves just to the right of the steps against the east wall where they could have a good vantage point but remain as obscure as possible.

The atmosphere was not that expected in a house of worship. The prevailing spirit seemed to be more like a town hall meeting, where people come to exchange news, mixed with the uneasy expectations of an election campaign headquarters, where they waited for developments to take place. The smatterings of conversation they were able to pick up ranged from some outrageous new tax being levied on imported perfumes to the drain on the Treasury from the never-ending construction costs of Herod's summer home at Masada. A home is one thing, but this monstrosity would house an entire city, it was said.

They were hesitant to draw attention to themselves by seeking out information about where and when various rabbis would be speaking. They chose to wait and be as selective as possible of whom they would ask questions, even though they had nothing but their instincts to guide them.

After a while three men entered the great courtyard and walked over to within a few feet of where Eric and Milcah stood. Two of them seemed to be priests or scribes, since they wore the same type of hooded robe that he had first seen on Ishmael as he peered into his cave on that fateful morning. The third man was tall, but frail and rather poorly dressed. He looked uncomfortable and out of place as his eyes darted nervously around the area. There was a brief conversation, then one of the priests left, leaving the other two men standing there.

Eric watched them for a moment. No conversation took place between them and soon the remaining priest moved a few feet away where he could get a better view of those entering the inner court at the far end.

An instinct that held only limited conviction told Eric that he might be able to get some information from the tall man. Signaling Milcah to remain where she was, he made his way through the crowd and stood next to him.

The man gave Eric a fleeting glance and abruptly turned his head away. It was the kind of gesture that does not encourage social conversation from strangers.

Eric chose to ignore this, and spoke quietly to him, "Excuse me. I have heard that a man called Jesus may speak here today. Do you know if it is true?"

The man jerked his head around as if he had heard a voice from the grave. His dark eyes bore the burdens of a hundred emotions, but the overriding one was fear.

He said nothing, and Eric was confused by his reaction.

"He is a teacher that someone told me may speak here today. I only wondered if you knew him."

"Who are you? Who sent you here?" The man seemed almost terror stricken.

"No one sent me. I am merely a stranger passing through Jerusalem and I have heard of this man's teachings. I only thought that you might know his whereabouts so that I could hear him speak."

"He will not be here today," he blurted out, then reacted as if he wanted to recall his words.

"How do you know that," Eric pressed.

"I know nothing. Go away! Leave me alone, I know nothing of this man!" He now seemed near panic.

Eric, still unable to understand the man's reaction, tried to say something to calm him down. "I'm sorry to have bothered you. I only thought that perhaps there was a programmed schedule of speakers that I was not aware of. Peace be with you."

His tortured eyes locked into Eric one more time, and then he turned away, clearly announcing that the conversation had been terminated. Eric drifted back to where Milcah was standing.

"Did you learn anything?" She asked.

"No," he replied, with his eyes still fixed upon the man's back, "except..."

Just then the other priest rejoined the two, and with a single gesture the three of them left to make their way into the Court of Women. In parting, the man flashed Eric one last, troubled glance, and then they disappeared into the crowd.

"Except what?" Milcah asked.

Eric's eyes were still fixed upon the place in the crowd where the men had disappeared.

"Except that I don't believe Jesus will come to the temple today."

"How could you know that? Did that man know him?"

"No, he said he didn't."

"Then how could you possibly know?"

"I don't know. All I have to go on is a weak hunch. But it's telling me now that we should use the passport Ben Yaier gave us to leave the city."

"But where will we go?"

"The place called the Mount of Olives."

There was a knock at the door. Ben Yaier quickly shoved the photographs he had been studying under the woven tablecloth and placed a water urn on top of them.

"Come in."

It was Yasmine.

"Excuse me, master, but General Favious has asked if you would consent to having the noon meal with him in his quarters."

A twinge of uneasiness came over Ben Yaier, for he and the commander of the Roman Legion shared few common interests that would prompt such an invitation.

"Tell the Commander that it would please me very much, and that I will join him shortly."

When Yasmine left, Ben Yaier hid the photos in a safer place. He felt certain that Favious had not extended his invitation for strictly social reasons. If it did have to do with Eric he wondered if he should lie, play ignorant, or tell the truth. The last alternative was not even worth considering. Even if he used the photographs to verify his story and they believed him it would only intensify the search, and God only knows what the consequences would be when they found him. He would have to play it by ear.

A servant girl led him through the living chambers out onto the balcony where Favious was reclining on a lounge, holding his head in his hands. He was a big man in his early fifties. A full head of hair was made to seem even whiter by his weathered face that bore a scar from his left eye to his ear; a memento from a campaign near Constantinople. His large, muscular arms bore evidence of a once superior physical condition than was now evidenced by his large stomach.

"Welcome, my friend. Come join me in some wine before we eat," Favious said in a warm tone, as he rolled his head in a circular motion.

"Thank you. I'm honored at your invitation."

"I'll say one thing for you Jews, you really know how to throw a feast. My head feels like a chariot ran over it."

"It has always amazed me how anything as sweet as a grape can turn into a roaring lion when it is fermented," Ben Yaier quipped.

"Well said, Scholar. Join me in a toast to fermentation." They both drank and there were a few seconds of silence as if neither of them were sure where to begin.

"So tell me, how was your journey? I understand you were in Alexandria," Favious broke the silence.

"Yes. I had heard of a new process developed there, which turns molten sand into a transparent material. They call it glass."

"Sand that you can see through? What do they use it for?"

"That part is still uncertain. They're still trying to mill it in sheet form, possibly to use in buildings to allow light in while keeping the wind and rain out."

"Interesting." Favious' interest perked up as the gears of his military mind engaged. "Does it have the strength to withstand the blow of a sword or battle axe?"

"I believe I can guess some of the applications you are thinking of, but alas, I'm afraid that a stone thrown by a child would shatter it."

"A pity," Favious said, and immediately lost interest in the subject. "So! What else of interest took place on your journey?"

Ben Yaier knew it was a loaded question, designed to draw him out. He decided to volunteer nothing and let Favious be specific if the conversation was being maneuvered around to Eric. "The confinement of a scholar's life, unlike that of a soldier, makes almost any journey an adventure. But at my age, every bump the wagon hit became a vivid memory."

Favious smiled a sipped some more wine. "We were delighted to give Herod the good news of your whereabouts on the day he returned from Masada. It seems that one of my officers encountered your caravan south of Hebron."

"Oh yes, a true officer and a gentleman. Had it not been for your invitation today, I would have requested an audience for the sole purpose of commending him to you personally."

"Some case of mistaken identity, I'm told."

Favious had worded it as a question rather than a statement. Ben Yaier could no longer avoid the subject.

"Yes. A man I had been traveling with who possesses knowledge of a new form of mathematics; it seems he vaguely matches the description of some fugitive your soldiers were seeking. An honest mistake. I'm sure your officer was only doing his duty."

"That's odd," Favious, mumbled with a large bite of cheese in his mouth, "now I'm confused. My officer was under the impression that the man was a bit dim-witted."

"Not a bit! But he has limited command of our language and it was natural for your captain to assume he was dim because he was slow in responding to his commands and questions."

"Yes, of course. I'm sure that would explain it," Favious said as he washed his cheese down with wine. "That would have placed your caravan in Hebron about four days ago, is that correct?"

"Yes, I believe that's about when we were there." Ben Yaier was beginning to feel quite uncomfortable as he realized that Favious had no intention of letting the matter drop.

Just then, two women brought in the food on a gold tray, and served them on the low tables besides their couches.

"Ah, wild quail," Favious said, "I promise you a treat now. My chef basted these in a sauce that is unlike anything you've ever tasted."

"It smells delicious," Ben Yaier said. He was tempted to ask for the recipe in an effort to divert the conversation, but he knew that such a frivolous tactic would be useless.

Favious ripped off a small leg of the fowl and stripped it in one bite. "We had another incident in Hebron the very day you were there."

"Oh?" Ben Yaier said.

"Yes. It appears that this same fugitive attacked an entire five-man patrol single-handed."

"Really! Surely, then, they took him into custody." Ben Yaier did his best to sound convincing.

"No. No, they didn't. Whoever this man is, he has the ability to handle himself remarkably well against superior odds. Some reports even go so far as to suggest that he possesses supernatural powers."

"I see!" Ben Yaier said. He was aware that Favious was watching him in an attempt to read any reaction his eyes might betray.

"There is a man here in the palace, a Pharisee who does some sort of investigative work for your priests, who was questioning this mysterious man when he and four of my soldiers were overpowered in a way that is still not clear to me. At any rate, the man, and the woman he was with, stole the soldiers' horses and fled." Still watching Ben Yaier's face, which remained inscrutable, he continued, "Two days later, the patrol in Hebron found the woman and were questioning her when he attacked them, putting three of them under a physician's care with broken bones."

"It's a most interesting story, General, but I suspect you have some reason for telling me all this other than mere dining conversation."

"We have taken three other men into custody that matched the description, but none of them proved to be the one we are looking for. It's merely a formality that I'm sure will come to nothing, but as long as this Pharisee, Saul, who could bear witness to the man, is here I'm sure you wouldn't mind arranging a meeting between him and your guest." There was a few second's pause. "I know it's ridiculous, but that way we can put the matter behind us," Favious said with an insincere laugh.

"Of course, General, I'm certain that he would be happy to comply with such a request. I'll arrange the meeting as soon as he returns."

"Returns?" Favious bellowed.

"Yes. Their stay here was only temporary. He and his wife had business in Ramallah, but they plan to return here before continuing on to Caesarea."

"I see," Favious said in a tone that more than hinted at suspicion of Ben Yaier's story. "Well then, I suppose it will have to wait until they return."

Favious tossed the half eaten carcass of the quail back onto the platter, dipped his fingers into a small golden bowl of water, and wiped his hands on a linen napkin. "I want to thank you for joining me on such a short notice. I wish we had more time to chat, but alas, duty calls and I must meet with some of my officers. With your Passover approaching, the population of Jerusalem has already doubled, which unfortunately calls for additional security."

"Of course." Ben Yaier accepted his dismissal gracefully. "Thank you for inviting me, and rest assured that I will contact you the moment my guests return."

"Yes, thank you."

Ben Yaier was nearly off the terrace when Favious called to him: "Ben Yaier, where was it you said that you first encountered these people?"

"I'm not sure that I did say, General, but to the best of my recollection it was in Asluj, forty kilometers or so south of Beersheba."

"Asluj," Favious repeated, and smiled a farewell.

Ben Yaier duplicated a similar stealthy smile and left the Commander still toying with his napkin. He was certain that Favious had not believed his story and that he had no intention of dismissing the matter. More than likely he would order a search of the palace, and then send out patrols to look for Eric and Milcah. Based upon the stories of their prior encounters with Eric, it was certain that the Roman soldiers would give little time to courtesy or negotiations if they thought they had found their suspects. He must get word to them.

Quickly he wrote a message explaining what had happened and warning Eric not to return to the palace. He dispatched Yasmine with instructions to look for them first in the temple. If he made no contact with them there he was to seek them out in the vicinity of the Mount of Olives. If he still failed to find them, he was to destroy the parchment before returning to the palace.

CHAPTER XVII

With the use of the Royal Seal provided by Ben Yaier, Eric and Milcah had no problem leaving the city through the temple gate on the eastern wall. The road to Bethpage dipped down into the Kidron Valley before starting its climb up the slope of the Mount of Olives.

The road leading up the hill was alive with activity. Visitors from all the provinces of the Jewish nation had returned to Jerusalem to celebrate the Passover. Thousands of campsites were spread over the landscape as far as one could see. From a distance it gave the appearance of a city under siege. Like a giant ant farm, lines of travelers made their way in and out of the Holy City's gates past Roman guards made sloppy in their inspection duties by the crush of traffic.

Eric was growing concerned that the rapidly approaching darkness would hamper their efforts to locate where Jesus and his followers were camped. There was neither time nor need for caution now as they stopped and pressed incoming travelers for information. Most of those they asked seemed to have no idea who they were talking about, while others had no time to give any answer at all. They finally met one older man hobbling along, trailing a small goat on a rope who at first ignored their inquiry. But after passing them he turned back and pointed up the hill saying only one word, "Gethsemane."

"Thank you," Eric yelled, but the old man had already turned and was scampering down the hill, dragging his protesting goat.

"Come on," Eric grabbed Milcah by the hand.

They had no more than turned around to start up the hill when they heard a voice calling out from the crowd. "Edh-rik."

It sounded like his name, but how could that be? Then it came again, and as their eyes searched back down the road at the milling travelers they recognized Yasmine, fighting his way upstream like a salmon at spawning time.

"Edh-rik," he yelled one more time as they moved back to meet him.

"Yasmine, is anything wrong?" Eric asked anxiously.

Fighting to catch his breath and holding out the parchment he said, "My master told me to give you this."

Eric read it in the dim light that was still left of the day, and then handed it back to Yasmine.

"What is it Eric? What does it say?" Milcah asked.

"Ben Yaier may have bought us a little time, but we cannot return to the palace. Favious has asked that a meeting be arranged with Saul upon our return, which he told him would be in a few days. But he believes Favious is suspicious of his story."

"So what do we do?" Milcah asked.

"We do what we came to do," he replied, after a moment's reflection.

"Yasmine, tell your master that if anything should happen, under no circumstances should he claim anything except that I deceived him as to who I really am. I want no suspicion to fall on him."

Yasmine looked puzzled at what Eric was telling him, but asked no questions. He said simply, "I will tell him what you have said."

"Thank you. Now go quickly, and bury the parchment someplace where you will not be seen."

"I will do as you say." He turned and headed back to Jerusalem.

About a hundred feet ahead there was a path leading up the hill away from the main road. Some of the campsites had tents, but others had only blankets and cooking utensils on the ground. Many of the women were already preparing the evening meal: the smoke from their fires filled the cooling desert air as night began to fall. In the distance could be heard the tinkling of a camel's bell, a baby crying, impatient for its mother's breast, children's laughter, and somewhere a shepherd playing on his flute.

Eric could feel his adrenaline mounting as he quickened his pace up the hill. There had never been anything in his life before that he could compare to the exhilaration he experienced now. He had never felt so alive, and yet the whole fantastic scene had the air of a capriciously realistic dream. What had seemed like a fantasy that one entertains just prior to drifting off to sleep now loomed before him as a promise. Somewhere out there, perhaps just a few moments away, was the Nazarene who, many would come to believe, could provide new life for a dying world.

It was a large hillside area with scattered clumps of trees. Darkness was beginning to surround them now, and their search became even more intense. They limited their investigation to the larger camps, as he knew there would be at least thirteen in the party. The people they questioned were no more able to help them than those on the road. The light from an increasing number of scattered fires made it a little easier to stay on the poorly defined path. They were getting more concerned now, for the further south they walked the more the campsites thinned out.

About fifty feet off the main path a lone figure sat in front of a lean-to, stirring something in a kettle that hung from a tripod over the fire. As they got closer they could see it was a woman in her fifties. The dancing flames cast unflattering shadows on her weather-aged face. They greeted her and asked if she might know the location of the camp of Jesus.

"Ask that one," she said without interrupting her stirring, but nodding her head in the direction of a lone hooded figure just leaving her camp. "He's one of them."

"Thank you, thank you very much," Eric said as he grabbed Milcah by the hand again and hurried to catch up with the person walking away from them.

"Excuse me," Eric shouted from a few feet away.

The man stopped and turned around.

"We're looking for the place where a man called Jesus is staying. That woman back there said that you know him."

"What is it you want from him?"

"Only to speak with him. We have traveled a very great distance to do so."

After some hesitation he said, "Our camp is that last fire you see there on the left." Then he added, "but the teacher will not be able to see you now, as he is in prayer and meditation."

The man turned his head so that the campfire revealed the face that had been shadowed by his hood. Eric couldn't place it a first, but he had seen the man somewhere before.

"I know you!" Eric said.

The man only stood there for a few seconds, then moved around to the other side so he could see Eric's face that had been silhouetted by the firelight behind him. Almost immediately, there was a change of expression in his eyes that told Eric that the man now also recognized him...but from where?

Then it came to him. "The temple. You were at the temple today," Eric said.

The man said nothing, but then that same fear that Eric had seen earlier returned to his face.

"Don't you recall? We spoke to each other there today."

"You have me mixed up with someone else. I tell you I was not at the temple today."

"But I'm sure it..."

"No! It was not me!" He cut off Eric's sentence. "The teacher will not be able to see you tonight." With that, he turned and hurried off in a different direction than he had been headed when they had stopped him.

Eric and Milcah were at a loss as they stood there and watched him hurry away into the darkness.

"Did we do something wrong, Eric? We seem to have upset him."

"I'm not sure," he said, as he stood rubbing his chin in a gesture of perplexity. "Come on." Still holding Milcah's hand they headed back to where the woman was sitting by the fire.

"But don't you want to go..." Milcah didn't finish the sentence but was pointing toward the campfire the man had indicated.

"In a minute. But first I want to check something out."

The woman was adding a few more twigs to the fire as they walked back into her camp. The fresh fuel made a crackling sound as it sent sparks dancing upward into the night air.

"Excuse me," Eric said, "but that man who was just here, do you know his name?"

She looked up from her kettle and said, "He is the one they call Judas."

There it was. Suddenly it all fell together. His behavior at the temple, the way he acted just now. The man had, this day, negotiated to commit the most infamous act of betrayal in the history of mankind. He was overcome with paranoia and obviously eating his guts out with guilt. Still, Eric could not help but wonder if that tortured soul had any idea just how far reaching the effects of his deed would be. Could he possibly imagine the part he had just played in changing the course of history? The taking of his own life a few days from now would at least bear evidence to the depth of his remorse.

"He truly is a blessed one of God," she said. "He has shown us much kindness and given us food."

"He has had a good teacher," Eric said. He thanked her again and they left.

Walking toward the place that Judas had indicated, Eric wondered if he should attempt to tell Jesus what Judas had done; warn him to go away from Jerusalem; do something to head off the impending disaster.

Then, like a Santa Ana wind blowing all the clouds away, the answer came to him and he recognized the folly of any thought of intervention. If the scriptures were true then Jesus knew that he would be betrayed. He knew that he would suffer and die, and that nothing in heaven or on earth, except his own choice, could or would change that.

Now they were close. Eric could make out figures moving around in the camp. Who were they? James, Matthew, Peter? It was beginning to happen to him again, the feeling of overpowering awe. It was like a computer being fed far beyond its capabilities but, in this case, the software was 'expectations'. Those figures moving about, performing menial chores, were nothing more than a group of confused students doing their best to understand what the man they were following was trying to say to them. None of them could conceive of what was about to happen to them, in their wildest dreams they could never imagine that they, themselves, would one day be declared Saints: that sculptors would carve statues and artists would conjure up images of them, and they would become objects of worship, contrary to the teachings of their Rabbi. They would, indeed be the charter members of one of the largest and least understood organizations the world would ever know. But from this vantage point they were just a group of men, like those in the other camps, trying to keep a fire going or repairing a broken sandal strap.

Men...they were only men, Eric kept insisting to himself in order to get his feelings of objectivity into balance as they drew closer to the camp.

What if one of these figures is Jesus, the thought suddenly occurred to him.

Then it started again, the knot in his stomach, the compulsion to verify his own physical presence in that time and place, the overpowering feeling of dream-like unreality, that he would surely awake at any moment. Was he really this close? Somewhere from the far corners of his inner self there was an inaudible voice reminding him that perhaps he shouldn't be there at all. For the first time he felt like an imposter, sneaking into someplace he didn't belong.

Knock it off, Stupid. Get a hold of yourself; you've come too far to turn back now. He gave himself silent commands.

They stopped a few feet away from three men and a woman who hadn't seen them yet. Eric took a deep breath, squeezed Milcah's hand, and walked up to the group.

190

They were greeted with warm, welcoming smiles.

"We were told that we could find a man called Jesus here," Eric said.

"He is here," one of the men answered, "up there." He pointed to a small path that led up through an outcropping of boulders, partially hidden by two olive trees. "But he is in prayer at present."

"May we wait? We have traveled a long way to speak to him."

The man who had spoken made a gesture for them to be seated.

"Have you eaten?" the woman asked.

Not until she asked did it occur to either of them that they had not eaten since morning.

"Thank you, we are hungry, and we can pay," Eric said.

The woman smiled warmly and said, "there is enough for all."

She left and returned in less than a minute with two large bowls of soup. A young girl that came back with her gave them bread and water. She spread a small swaddling cloth on the ground in front of them, served their evening meal, and left.

There was no coldness in the group, and Eric and Milcah did not sense any feeling other than being welcome. It was an act of consideration that they were left to enjoy their meal undisturbed. The only word spoken was a warm wish for them to "enjoy."

The simple meal provided a welcome relief, but when it was finished they both just sat there exchanging an occasional nervous smile. There was nothing to say because both knew what the other was thinking. For Eric, it was like waiting at a traffic signal at a desert crossroad; not traffic in either direction for as far as the eye could see but still the light never changed. The waiting grew more difficult with each passing second. There were probably rules or protocol he should follow, but what was churning inside him left no room for rules. He stood up and held out his hand to Milcah.

She rose and put her hand in his. There was no need to ask any questions.

Together they walked toward the trees and onto the path that led up the hill where Jesus was to be found. In a short distance they rounded a large boulder that could not be seen over. There, less than ten feet away sat the lone figure of a man with his back to them and the hood of his robe pulled over his head. The moon had not yet risen in the east, but one could feel that he sensed their presence.

Those explorers coming upon the Grand Canyon or Niagara Falls, the astronauts standing on the moon, the sum total of all the wonders that mankind had ever beheld would have paled in significance compared to the feelings that Eric was experiencing at that moment. The barely distinguishable outline of a man sitting in a non-descript desert wasteland would hardly seem awe-inspiring, but whoever had the greatest command of the written word would have found his pen inadequate to describe that moment.

Eric had no idea how long he and Milcah stood there, frozen. They might never have moved had not the figure, without turning, raised a hand and said, "Come."

They made their way forward and stood beside him.

"Please, I must talk to you," Eric managed to say.

The hooded figure turned slowly. Eric was unable to distinguish any of his facial features in the darkness, and Jesus said nothing to him. He then made a simple gesture, which invited them to come and sit beside him.

As they did so, Eric was finding it more and more difficult to maintain the objectivity he had convinced himself would be necessary if this moment should actually ever occur. Now that the moment was actually here it didn't matter to him how the rest of the world felt, or would feel, about this man. The world would soon kill him. Most of the world would deny him. Those claiming to follow him, for the most part, would be hypocrites and liars, misleading millions, building mighty buildings to house their dungeons. They would split into hundreds of fragments, each one shouting to the masses, "Come, follow me. I understand him best. This is the way."

It didn't matter. None of it mattered. This was his moment... His moment. What to do with it? He felt himself going blank, out of control. What was happening? All the burning questions he had rehearsed a thousand times in his mind were blending together so none of them alone could possibly make any sense.

Say something, he screamed silently to himself. Panic had replaced the serenity he was feeling only a few seconds ago. He sat there dumbfounded. Perhaps it really was a dream, the kind where you try to scream but no sound comes out.

Time had stopped for him. Time, that inexplicable, wondrous moving thing that he had labored a lifetime over, through thousands of equations, had suddenly imprisoned him. Could fate possibly be that ironic?

Jesus reached out his hand and touched him gently on the shoulder.

Not only did time begin to move again, but also he felt a surge of indescribable contentment flow through his entire body. He could function now and he was like a wolf just released from a trap that takes no time to ponder how the jaws were sprung, but knows only that the pain has stopped and it is free to move. So it was with Eric. Giving no consideration to what it was that released him from his emotional prison he, like the wolf, proceeded without question or gratitude to ask, "Do you know who I am?"

"I know that you are not who you represent yourself to be," the answer came.

"I didn't mean to misrepresent myself. I just didn't know how else to reach you. They wouldn't have understood."

"I have no need to deceive others when I speak to my Father in prayer," he answered.

Even though Eric understood the underlying meaning of that statement he chose to lay it to one side and ask, "Forgive me, Jesus, but is there no hope for those who cannot find their answers in prayer?"

'There are but two things under the Sun—Good and Evil. It is within all mankind to have the right to choose."

"But is it wrong, then, to question?" Eric said.

"There is no wrong in seeking the answers to what you do not know, but ask first for understanding, then step out of the way. Do not attempt to assist the one whom you have asked with your own preconceived thoughts, for surely what you will get if you do will be your own answers."

"But Lord, I have asked for answers to those things that I don't understand. I have asked many times. I just don't receive any answers."

"You call me Lord, but yet you don't know why. Behold, am I not flesh and blood like you? Why then should you believe the answers I might give to your questions?"

"But I would believe you," Eric insisted.

"Is the messenger, then, more important than the message? Is the joy of truth less joyous when delivered by a child, rather than a man of high regard?"

"But if only I could understand why God allowed some things to happen the way they do, perhaps then..." his voice trailed off as if he felt himself becoming repetitive.

"Man will intellectualize the wisdom of the Father even unto death, and still not gain understanding. For man is of such a nature that should he fly to the moon the world would be awed by his accomplishments, but meditate little on the One who placed the moon in the sky."

The thought hit Eric, whether Jesus was indicating that he knew about him and the future with this reference to a man on the moon, or was he merely using a parable? He chose to make no comment.

"The things you seek are not hidden from me." He surprised Eric with the statement.

"Do you mean that you already know the questions that I would ask?"

"Are you not concerned with the question: Where is the justice in all mankind inheriting the sins of Adam and Eve? Do you not question that if it were Lucifer who went against

God and deceived them with a lie, would justice not have been better served with his annihilation?"

Eric felt sure now, though it brought him no discomfort, that Jesus was able to read his thoughts.

"Yes, yes... Please forgive me, but I would not be honest if I didn't say that there would have been more justice in that solution."

"It is only the way of man to have his will prevail by means of his power. The ability to destroy another proves nothing except that ability. The right or wrong of the matter remains unproven. The rebellion in Eden was not only of Satan and the two souls of the flesh, as all the Angels in Heaven to whom choice was given, just as it was given to man, witnessed the confrontation. Thus this act of defiance exploded to a universal scale, as many choose to follow the Wicked One. For them there will be no salvation. For, like Adam and Eve, they were created perfect, without sin, and all things were given unto them, just as was given to them the right to choose right from wrong, good from evil.

"As for the descendants of Adam, they would all be born in sin, as it is impossible to produce something perfect out of that which is imperfect. The Father provided a means for their salvation because of His love for them. The plan was later revealed to His servant Moses, whom He commanded to write. But most men will read with their eyes and listen with their ears, and not seek understanding with their hearts. The seas of humanity that witness and become victims of the miseries brought onto the world by the false guardians of their souls will cry out in protest that 'No God of love could rule in such a manner.'"

"But Lord, what else can mankind think amidst all the suffering? Untold millions die in forgotten wars that solve nothing. Children starve. Pestilence, drought and disease cause crying and agony the world over."

"Even though the hearts of men have turned against Him, the Father takes no joy in their suffering."

"Surely then, God has the power to change that which man cannot! It is no secret that the powers of this world still operate out of greed and fear of that which they don't understand, which only leads to more chaos. Lord, if man cannot solve his own problems, where then, is it all to end?"

"It will end as it began, but then there will be no end."

Eric just looked at him and tried to understand the meaning of his words. His eyes were now adjusting to the darkness and, as the moon in its third phase began rising over the hill behind him, he was able to distinguish the features of the face that had been hidden in the shadow of the hood. The face was not one of frail sadness that has been depicted in so many artists' renderings. It was a strong, handsome face, almost beautiful. The eyes contained the wonders and the wisdom of the Universe, soft and kind, yet with the power to pierce into one's very soul and strip it of its innermost secrets. But there was no threat, for they bore only love, with just the slightest hint of frustration, such as you might expect to see in the eyes of the only rational inmate somehow unjustly committed to an insane asylum.

Unable to resolve the meaning of what Jesus had said, Eric asked, "Do you mean by that, that God will create two new people?"

Those magnificent eyes fixed on Eric for a few seconds. Then, as if he had made an inner decision, Jesus began to speak.

"It was God's will for man to be perfect and to dwell on a perfect earth where all things were provided, a world without sickness, pain, fear or death. He asked only that man should have no other God before him. Sin entered the world through jealousy, when the beloved Lucifer was given the position of guardian of God's newest and weakest creations. Lucifer wanted them to worship him, so he put forward the lie that they would surely not die if they ate of the fruit in opposition to God's instructions. It was this act that brought forth the universal confrontation between God and the forces of evil.

"Lucifer, who is Satan, became the ruler of things here on earth. It was at this same time that the Father put forth his plan for the redemption of mankind, so that it might regain the things stolen from it by its parents. My Father would use the blood of his Son as a ransom to purchase this sin that all had inherited, so that death would have no hold on them.

"At the end of Satan's time, after the battle of Armageddon, those who have tasted death will be resurrected back to life in a sinless condition to inherit a cleansed earth, no longer influenced by the Evil One, for he will be locked away in the Abyss for a millennium. It will be during that period that mankind, now repurchased and no longer with sin, will regain the perfection that once belonged to its original parents in Eden.

"They will be given the same freedom to choose a relationship with the Father or, once again, to be lured by Satan to a certain and final destruction when he is released for a short period of time after the thousand years. Those loving the ways of God will gain everlasting life. It is God's perfect love that will buy back life for man."

Eric sat spellbound. He felt for the first time in his life that he was really listening. But the words! Could they really be true? It all sounded so unsophisticated. He could just picture the amused grins of a group of intellectuals at a cocktail party arming themselves with arrows of sarcastic rebuttal, should Jesus somehow show up in a Brooks Brothers suit and present them with this same message. Why pick on modern intellectuals, he thought. Jesus risked daily rejection in a world two thousand years less sophisticated.

Eric eagerly took the opportunity to press for more information. "You spoke of Armageddon. Will man really destroy himself in a global war?"

"Man could do nothing but destroy man without discrimination. Armageddon will be God's war in heaven and on earth. Those who walk in His way will not perish."

"When will this happen, Lord?"

"Signs will be given man near the time, but even if you knew the exact hour it would not serve you, for there is no salvation in knowledge alone."

Jesus then looked at Milcah who had been listening just behind Eric, but had not spoken a word. He held out his hand and said, "Come forth, woman." The command was gentle.

Milcah seemed mesmerized as she slid closer without rising. It was almost as if she was floating, since her movement made no sound. She sat directly in front of him. His eyes were fixed on hers.

"As for you," he said softly, "do you have any questions you would ask of me?"

"No Lord, I have none," she answered in a voice that was barely more than a whisper.

"And why is it that you call me Lord?"

"My heart tells me that it is true," she replied, simply.

"You, then, have the greatest gift of all."

Then he turned to Eric and said, "There are those who feel they need to prove God's existence. Was there nothing learned from the miracles performed by God through Moses? Were they not witnessed by the multitudes that he led out of Egypt? Then, even after such a display, did they still not hammer a god out of gold so that they might see a thing they could worship? Is God, then, to become a magician, performing acts so that man will be reminded of his presence? The intellect will question always, but the wise man need only behold the petal of a flower and know that he need not question."

With that Jesus rose and said, "I must pray now, for my work is not yet finished."

He walked a few feet away then turned around and spoke these final words, "You have heard things this night even beyond that revealed to my loved ones here on earth, because the time has not yet arrived for them to understand. For you, Traveler, it is different. Still, it may be that your quest to prove those things unseen will rob you of seeing all that is truth and leads to life. If you feel in your heart that there is a Higher Power, then surrender to it. Let it be your guide and let your life become your message to others. The choice is yours."

He turned again and followed the path up the hill, disappearing into the shadows of the trees.

Eric and Milcah remained sitting there and said nothing for several minutes. Finally Eric spoke in a near whisper, "I am full, yet I am empty. God help me."

Milcah tenderly placed her hand in his and said, "I believe that He will."

He turned slowly and looked at her. Even in the darkness her face was glowing with a kind of beauty he had never seen in her before. She smiled at him and gently squeezed his hand. He never would have believed that it was possible for a man to pinpoint the exact moment when he truly fell in love, but he was wrong. Right at that moment, looking at her, he knew without any doubt that he loved this woman more than life itself. He rose to his feet, and she with him, still holding his hand.

"Come, we must go," he said.

"Where are we going?"

"Out of harm's way. If Ben Yaier's hunch is correct, the area around Jerusalem will be swarming with Roman soldiers looking for us. We'll make our way south, staying off the main road, and get you back into the safety of your father's house."

"And you, Eric, what will you do?"

"We'll talk later. I have much to think and even pray about, but now we must go."

CHAPTER XVIII

Felix Renthroe closed the file cabinet drawer and was going through his pockets for his office key when the phone rang.

The voice at the other end offered no greetings, only a direct question, "Felix, how far away are you from the nearest pay phone?"

"Chris, is that you?" He was caught off guard by the abruptness.

"Yes, but I don't want to talk now. How long will it take you to get to a pay phone?"

"About five minutes. Why?"

"Go there and call that number back to me. Then wait there. I'll go to another pay booth here and call you back within ten minutes."

"Still don't trust our scrambler, do you? Must be hot!"

"Ten minutes," Chris repeated, and hung up.

Felix did as Chris requested, then just stood there in the booth of the nearly empty lobby waiting for the phone to ring. It was Good Friday, and except for the Security people, who were everywhere, most of the employees in the Central intelligence Agency Headquarters had taken off earlier in the afternoon. The row of elevator doors that were normally opening and closing with their heavy traffic loads remained closed except for an occasional lone passenger.

Felix jumped a little when the phone rang. The sound, that might have gone unnoticed in the normally busy lobby, sounded like a fire drill in the empty hall.

"Chris?"

"Hi, Felix. Sorry about the cloak and dagger stuff, but you told me how tight a wrap the President wants placed on this thing."

"Hey, I'm impressed. I didn't know you knew that old pay phone routine."

"I think I saw it on T.V."

"So, Chris, what have you got? We're dead in the water at this end."

"I would have called you right away but we wanted to check something out first."

"What are you talking about? Check what out first?"

"It's back. We've got it."

"What? Say that again."

"The capsule. It's back."

"You mean..."

"Yeah."

"Good Lord! Where is it?"

"Right now it's sitting in a pasture out near Riverside, close to a little town called Mira Loma."

"What the hell is it doing out there?"

"We don't know. We don't know a lot of things, because we still don't know what we're dealing with. Some school kids found it, but they didn't go inside it. Right now it's all sealed off by the Sheriffs Department and the C.H.P., Waiting for you guys. I didn't want to contact your Los Angeles office; thought I'd better leave that up to you."

"Where's Corbett now?"

"We don't know."

"What do you mean?"

"I mean we don't know where he is."

"Chris, how in hell could that thing get out there in a field all by itself?"

"Well, that part we think we do have figured out. To keep it simple, it doesn't appear to require the presence of an operator."

"Chris," Felix took a deep breath, "I've got a select group of people calling me on a daily basis. Not the least of these is the President of the United States. They all want to know the same thing: what the hell is going on? So please, let me ask a few basic questions. Where did the damn thing go? How does it work? And what happened to Corbett?"

"Look, Felix, I know where you're coming from and the pressure you've got on you, but I can only help you with

201

what we know so far. I mentioned earlier that I had delayed calling you. The reason for that was that we wanted to verify the authenticity of something we found in the capsule."

"What are you talking about?"

'It wasn't completely empty. Do you recall my saying that we thought we were missing a final set of equations back when we first found out about this thing?"

"Yes."

"They were in the capsule."

"Is that what you had to verify?"

"No. Perry is working on those right now, but that's going to take some time. There was something else."

"For God's sake, Chris, what? What else was there?"

"A photograph."

"A photograph?"

"Yes. That's the thing we had to run through the lab. It is positively authentic and un-retouched. I asked Perry to have it examined and he took it to a Professor Rubens there at the University; he's an internationally recognized authority on Hebrew history and culture."

"Now wait a minute, Chris, before you go any further. If you found this capsule abandoned out in some field, isn't it possible that Corbett found some way of getting it out of there and then for some reason or other got panicky and decided to just dump the thing?"

"No, Felix, that isn't what happened."

"Well, what am I supposed to tell the President, Chris? That this guy just took off with our hardware for a couple of weeks and sent it back with a picture post card in it."

"Hey Felix, lighten up. We've all been up tight about this thing. We're working as fast as we can to get you answers with the limited number of people we can let in on the research."

"Ah hell, I'm sorry, Chris. I just haven't been able to think straight since I last saw you. I've never dealt with so many unknowns in my life." He inhaled another big breath of air and let it out slowly. "Did this thing really go someplace and come back again?"

"We're convinced it did. I don't know how long it will be until Perry is finished with the equations, but the photograph really doesn't leave any doubt."

"You mentioned a Professor Rubens. What's this a picture of?"

"Corbett, standing in front of a gate outside of Jerusalem."

"So, I've had my picture taken there too. What does that prove?"

"Before the twelfth century?"

"What?"

"We have positive proof that the photograph was taken before the twelfth century, probably much before."

There was silence on the phone.

"Felix, are you there?"

Finally the answer came, "Yes, I'm here. How can you be sure about the year the photograph was taken, Chris?"

"We can't be sure about the exact year, but Rubens said it had to do with some lions that were carved on the gate sometime in the twelfth century and that weren't there at the time this picture was taken. Of course, Perry couldn't tell him anything, but if you think you're going crazy you should see poor Professor Rubens."

"I can imagine... where do you think Corbett is now, Chris?"

"We don't know for sure, but we have a pretty good guess based upon the note that was with the photo. It was written on papyrus."

"What's that?"

"It's a material made from a water plant, the same thing the Dead Sea Scrolls were written on."

"My God, Chris, do you really think..." He stopped, unable to finish his own thought.

"Yes, I do." Chris answered the unfinished question.

"Does the note tell us anything?"

"I'm afraid the answer to that is going to depend entirely upon the person reading it."

"What's that supposed to mean?"

"I mean that people like you and me, and the President, and all the shoe clerks who work every day, in whatever capacity, with the nuts and bolts of the machinery that runs this old world, are likely to find ourselves too busy with our wrenches and oil cans to place much validity in the ramblings of some egghead that simply isn't a mechanic like the rest of us."

"O.K., Chris, I think I've got your point, but even so, the fact remains that I have to deal with reality. Reality dictates that, in a short period of time, I'm going to have to report to the 'head mechanic' on this side of the world and tell him something." There was more dead air between them. "What does Corbett have to say, Chris?"

"I've got a copy with me. Do you have a recorder?"

"No, just read it. I'll get that later."

"It reads, 'I have given much thought to the folly of attempting to say in a few words those things that I thought would benefit mankind, based on my recent experience. I know now that the true folly would have been to try to put that experience into a million words. My words would mean nothing. Those words of any worth have already been written. Like much of the world, I read those words with hope, blended with skepticism. I sought confirmation. Therein lies the greatest folly of all.

"'From Cain's simple stick to our hydrogen bomb, man has demonstrated little other than his ability to build a bigger stick. And it will surely fall someday, left to man.

"'The truth is written. The promise is made. God willing that I, and anyone reading this, will find the way to accept it.

"'Signed, Eric Corbett'"

Again there was dead air. Finally Felix said, "That's it?"

"That's it," Chris confirmed.

"What are we dealing with here, Chris, some sort of religious nut?"

"That will be up to you, the President, and all of those top mechanics to decide, Felix. But one final personal thought..."

"What's that?"

"I hope you'll all do some reading, and maybe even say a little prayer. Then just hope, for God's sake - make that, for mankind's sake - that you don't bury something that the rest of the world should hear about.